EDGE OF DARKNESS

GREGORY DELAURENTIS

This is a work of fiction. The events, situations and locations described here are imaginary. The settings and characters are fictitious and not intended to represent specific places or living persons.

EDGE OF DARKNESS

ISBN: 978-0-9891857-5-2

To sleepless nights. A close friend who helped finish this work night after night.

GLITTER-GUN

The street was empty, and the shops in the small Vermont town looked dark and lonely. Only a few street lamps illuminated the tightly packed brick and vinyl siding storefronts that lined both sides of the wide cobblestone street. A gibbous moon hung lazily among the clouds overhead.

Willie Hamilton, dressed in tight-fitting jeans that were torn at the knees, calf-high cowboy boots, and a black distressed leather jacket, made his way down the sidewalk, glancing briefly into the shop windows as he passed. In one, a clothing store, mannequins dressed jauntily for a tennis game stared back at him, frozen in mid-motion.

The early fall evening was cool and gusty, scattering dust and dry leaves with enough force to send a speck of something into Willie's eyes, causing him to flinch momentarily. Recovering from the unwelcome distraction, he surveyed the deserted street, devoid of both people and vehicles. Satisfied that he was unobserved, he stopped in front of a jewelry store with a brightly lit neon sign and a placard on the door that read open. So as not to draw the attention of anyone inside, he turned the doorknob stealthily, and used his shoulder to nudge the door open without making a sound. Once inside, he shut the door behind him, and turned the placard around to read closed. Then he reached up to the pull chain for the neon sign and gave it a yank to turn it off.

To the left and the right of the front door were velvet-lined display cases—all empty. Their contents had undoubtedly been collected for the day and held for safekeeping in a vault located in the back office, which is where, Willie believed, he would find Trip Hepner. Listening intently, he moved silently toward the back of the store, until he started hearing the sounds of movement. He headed in their direction until he came to the doorway of the office, where he encountered his quarry bent over and peering into his waist-high safe, seemingly oblivious to the intruder's entry.

"Trip," Willie said sharply.

Hepner's body jerked and he whirled about, his face pale and glistening with sweat. He straightened his crooked glasses with a finger, while with his other hand he absently reached up to smooth down the hair on the top of his head. When he realized it was someone he knew, he gave a sigh of relief. "What's the matter with you?"

"Just playing. Shit, Glitter-Gun, have a sense of humor. I just wanted to catch you off guard. What are you up to there?" Willie asked, leaning against the threshold.

"Putting away the inventory like I do every day."

"Was it a good day?"

"Good enough," Trip said flatly, as he turned around to pick up where he left off. "So, what do you want, Willie?"

"I wanted to talk to you about something," he said, his thin lips parting in a toothy grin. His buzz-cut hairstyle was complemented by facial hair that formed a five o'clock shadow, but he looked more scruffy than fashionable. His clear blue eyes were intent on Hepner.

Hepner, his back to Willie, did not cease from his labor. "Go ahead—shoot."

"Kat and I want to cash out."

Trip stopped loading the safe and stood up slowly. "Did I hear you right? You want to cash out?" He turned around to read Willie's face, but with the light in the room was so dim, all he could see of him was one large shadow.

"Yeah," Willie replied.

"You're not talking about the conflict diamonds, are you?" Trip stepped closer to Willie, to face him squarely.

"I'm not talking about *all* of them, of course. I'm just talking about our cut."

"Your cut?"

"Yeah, mine and Kat's."

"You know that isn't wise, don't you?"

Instead of answering right away, Willie stepped deeper into the room to inspect a framed photograph on the wall of Hepner with Michael Gillette, the mayor of the town. Finally he spoke. "I know it'll be dangerous. The heat is still all over the case. You guys told us that over and over again, but we'll be careful."

"What do you mean by *we*?"

"Kat is with *me* now, Glitter-Gun." Willie's reflection in the glass of the photograph beamed like the proud father of a newborn.

Trip Hepner walked his sizable bulk across the room and over to his desk, sitting down heavily in the chair. Clearly uneasy, he started in again, stroking his greasy hair. "And what do you intend on doing with your share of six million dollars' worth of diamonds?"

"I want to take them to New York and fence them."

Hepner shook his head in disbelief. "Do you actually think it'll be just that easy? They're still too hot, Willie, and you have to find the right people willing to deal in unregistered diamonds. You can't do that. The only thing you'll do is lead the police right to your front door. And if they get to you, they get to all of us."

"I don't believe you anymore." Willie turned away from the photo to stand on the other side of the desk, looking down at Hepner. "Do you really think another two years are going to change anything?"

"Five years are better than three, my friend."

Willie scowled as he said, "I can't wait that long, Glitter-Gun. I want my share *now*."

"What's changed? What's going on now that wasn't before?"

"I've got some things to take care of… not that it's any of your business."

"Things like—Katherine?" Trip asked.

Willie went silent, rather than reveal his anger and frustration at being challenged like this.

"I don't know what to tell you." Hepner shrugged his shoulders helplessly.

"Okay, then… can you at least front us a couple of hundred thousand dollars in the meantime?"

Trip shook his head grimly. "I'm sorry, Willie. I can't. I just don't have that kind of cash lying around."

"But you're around jewelry every single day."

Hepner laughed heartily. "You don't understand. All these diamonds are negative inventory—when I *sell* them I'll have money. They're on consignment."

Willie didn't like being laughed at. It was time to cut to the chase. "Then take me to where you have the blood diamonds stashed, and I'll just take our share."

Willie's voice was no longer civil—it betrayed a hard edge. The change in tone didn't go unnoticed by Trip, who surreptitiously moved his leg away from where it was blocking the right-hand desk drawer that contained his .38-caliber Smith &Wesson. He was pretty certain that he wouldn't have to use it. He and Willie went way back together, buddies since high school. They weren't very close, but still thought of themselves in the very least as friends.

On the other hand, one could never be too certain about anyone—no matter how long the acquaintance—especially when large sums of money were at stake. Plus, Willie might have previously tanked up on liquid courage, which could lead to risky behavior. So sometimes just displaying a weapon could inspire a person to change their direction entirely. Besides, Trip reflected, Willie did sound a little "off," although he couldn't be certain that he'd been drinking.

In the meantime, Willie was planning his next move, his eyes wandering the room and finally falling on the heavy metal and porcelain desk lamp positioned between himself and Hepner.

"I want you to get your ass in gear and get me my diamonds right now, Glitter-Gun," Willie demanded in a menacing tone.

"That's not going to happen," Hepner firmly replied.

When he heard the flat refusal, Willie surged forward in

a blind rage, reaching across the desk for Hepner, who slid open his drawer, snatched the gun, and stood up—pointing it directly at Willie, who by now was nearly at his side. After a beat, Willie plowed into him, grabbing for the gun. Hepner wasn't prepared for the full frontal attack, and he fell backward, his finger jammed down on the trigger as he fell, causing the gun to go off. The bullet drilled a hole in the desk. Trip struggled against Willie, who was now straddling him, both men grappling for the weapon. Once Willie got a solid grip on Hepner's hand, he slammed the back of it hard against the linoleum several times until the gun clattered across the floor.

When he heard the noise, Trip reacted with a new urgency. He threw a left cross that caught Willie on the chin and knocked him sideway, which gave him the opportunity to get out from under him. As Hepner sat up, he was able to push Willie all the way off. After scrambling into a crouching position, Willie managed to grab the desk lamp. He stood up and swung it, catching Hepner across the temple, and shattering the lamp. The sheer momentum of the blow spun Hepner around, sending him down again. Without the lamplight, the room was illuminated only by the feeble light from inside the safe and the hallway.

"Don't make me hurt you more, Glitter-Gun," Willie said as he went to retrieve the Smith & Wesson from where it had landed earlier.

"Fuck you, Willie," Hepner said as he tried to stand up.

"This is already heading in a direction you don't want to go in. Do yourself a favor and make this easy on yourself. I'm not leaving until I get those diamonds," Willie said, pointing the gun at Hepner.

Using his desk for support, Trip stood up, the blood running from a gash on his forehead where Willie had struck him with the lamp.

Still pointing the gun at Trip's chest, Willie repeated his demand. "I'm going to tell you one last time—I want my share."

Hepner was dizzy and out of breath, and had to lean heavily on the edge of his desk to keep himself upright. Although he could see the weapon aimed at him in the semidarkness, he still didn't think Willie would use it. His 'friend' was no killer. But then again, Willie had never assaulted him before—so maybe the rules had changed after all.

Willie studied his opponent for a few moments, wondering what his next move would be. Still clutching the desk, Hepner's face was largely lost in shadow, not giving away much in the way of a clue. Nonetheless, Willie had the strong sense that Trip wasn't taking him seriously enough, probably counting on his past performance, assuming he was either too weak or too stupid to do anything drastic. But drastic measures were called for now, he thought. He had to show Hepner that he meant business.

Willie walked toward him and hit him sharply against the side of his jaw with the flat side of the pistol. The blow sent Hepner careening from his desk, crashing into a nearby table and chair as he lost his balance.

"Where are my diamonds, Glitter-Gun? I'm tired of you sitting on them and acting like you're the boss of me," Willie said as he came toward him, the muzzle of the gun trained on his opponent.

Lying amid the rubble, Trip raised himself into a sitting position. His head was throbbing and he spat out blood from the side of his mouth. "Have you gone fucking insane, Willie?"

An incensed Willie rushed at Hepner, delivering a crushing kick to his side that had him rolling across the floor groaning in pain.

"Where are the diamonds?!" Willie shouted down at him.

Hepner shifted his body so he was on his back. Despite the agony of every move, he managed to sit up again. Finally, after taking a deep breath, he growled back, "You'll get them over my dead body."

Katherine was parked on the sidewalk of the deserted street, having arrived sometime after Willie had entered the shop. She squirmed uncomfortably in the driver's seat, watching nervously for someone to come along and ask her what was she doing there—sitting in Willie Hamilton's 1962 green and white Ford pickup in the middle of the night. Even worse, what if that someone was Labrec Carville—the chief of police—who might lean in through the window and ask her if she was screwing William, and were they an item now?

Katherine shook her head in disgust. She was tired of the gossip and the small-town busybodies who seemed to be everywhere, especially at the most inconvenient times. Then she remembered why she was there, and focused her attention on the dimly lit windows of Trip Hepner's shop. Maybe the *plan* wasn't such a good idea. After all, Trip was a shady individual, very crafty and distrustful of others.

Of course, William—or Willie, as his friends called him—was not exactly the epitome of virtue either. His criminal career had started at the tender age of fifteen when he began stealing cars.

Although he was industrious in his pursuit of criminal activities, he was usually caught sooner or later because of some significant blunder. Since more often than not he exercised poor judgment, she wondered how good he would be at negotiation.

Katherine sat lost in thought for a moment more, until she spied William emerging from Hepner's shop. In a few long strides he crossed the cobblestone street and opened the driver's-side door. The door protested with a metallic screech as he swung it open and stepped up into the vehicle. After gently nudging Katherine into the passenger seat, he slipped in beside her and slammed the door shut.

"How did it go?" she asked, anxiously scanning Willie's T-shirt and dark jacket for signs of a struggle.

"Not all that good. He wasn't very cooperative. Or not as much as I thought he'd be." Willie leaned forward to turn the key in the ignition.

"So what happened?"

"He wasn't too helpful, that's all," Willie said noncommittally, as he drove the truck off the curb and into the street, headlights flaring.

"So what do we do now? Do we know where the diamonds are?" Katherine persisted, twisting around in her seat to lean back against the door, which was when she noticed the dark red flecks on William's face and on his T-shirt. She reached up to switch on the dome light, which bathed the two of them in its harsh glow. William came into full focus then, splattered with blood across his face, hands, T-shirt, and even his leather jacket. It took a minute before the full import of the sight sunk in.

"Did you kill Trip?" she gasped.

"I don't know," he said angrily. "I think so." Willie kept his eyes straight ahead, as he negotiated the twists and turns in the road.

"You think so?" Katherine repeated, sounding breathless. "What do you mean, you *think* so?"

"Let's just say that he wasn't too quick about telling me where the stuff was, so I had to coax it out of him. He was stubborn until bones started to break."

"You broke his bones?" Katherine was alarmed.

"Beating him up wasn't enough. He took it too well."

"He must be dead then." Her voice sounded small and distant as she reached up to turn off the courtesy light. "He must be dead because you would know if you left him alive."

"He—he threatened me. Threatened to report me to the police for assaulting him. With my record, that means several years in prison just for punching him around. Think about what would happen to our plan if I spent the next five to ten years in prison." He glanced at her briefly to see her reaction.

Katherine paused, trying to fathom what happened and where she fit in. What should she do now? This was supposed to be easy. Trip was just supposed to hand over the diamonds. Now they had no diamonds, no money—just a murder on their hands. She closed her eyes for a moment, wondering in retrospect why she agreed to be a part of this. What made her think that Willie could hold a civil conversation with someone not willing to give him what he wanted? But usually his clumsy efforts at cajoling someone merely ended in embarrassment, not homicide. Even if he did fear the idea of prison when Trip threatened to file charges, what kind of solution is murder? She shivered at the thought.

"So, now what?" she asked. "What *did* he tell you?"

"That they're at his beachfront home near Lake Dunmore, just a few miles north of here."

"Did he happen to say where *exactly* he hid the diamonds in the house?"

Willie swallowed hard before answering, "I think he died before he could tell me."

"You *think* he died before he could tell you? Where were *you*, in the next room?"

"He's DEAD, alright!" Willie struck the steering wheel with the flat of his hand.

Katherine fell silent.

REMEMBERING FATHER

Kevin Whitehouse was thinking how lucky he was to have a window seat, as he looked out at the final approach of the tiny Cessna 402 just before it landed at the Rutland Southern Vermont Regional Airport. The world below was a green carpet of bristling trees and grasslands, abruptly ending where the chalk white bands of landing strips crisscrossed each other, bordered by diminutive white hangars.

Suddenly, the plane banked sharply, its engines clearly revving now, as if straining to keep to the skies. Kevin clutched the ends of his armrests to steady himself. He could tell from the gasps of his fellow passengers that the tension level had risen sharply inside the small aircraft. Kevin chose to sit in the back because he'd heard that most people who survived plane crashes had seats in the rear section. While he knew this strategy probably had more application to larger aircraft, he still felt better sitting where he did.

The pilot, with a voice as cool as ice water, informed them that they were about to land.

The Cessna leveled off, rose as if riding the swell of a

wave, and then dropped—causing stomachs to rise. Kevin turned to the young woman seated on his right and managed a strained smile. She returned it with a tortured one.

Kevin looked out the window again, the distant trees rising up at them as the craft dropped rapidly to the ground. Then he heard whirring sounds and a thumping behind and beneath the fuselage. He sat back, leaning his head on the headrest and closing his eyes, as the shock of touchdown rushed up and down his frame. When the nose gear struck the strip with a screech, Kevin breathed again.

The Cessna taxied down the runway, then turned toward the hangars and the airport gate. There was the metallic sound in the cabin of seat belts being unlocked, and then people began to rise from their seats. But they quickly returned to them again when they heard the pilot's voice over the loudspeaker instructing them to stay seated until the plane stopped moving.

When it finally came to a full stop, the pilot, first divesting himself of some of his gear, opened the exit window on his left. He leaned out, braced his arms on the frame for support, and in one long step climbed onto the wing of the aircraft. The passengers waited patiently for the cabin door to drop after the pilot opened it from the outside, and filed out in an orderly fashion after he stepped aside to let them off.

Kevin lagged behind, remaining seated when the young woman next to him rose to disembark. When the plane was almost empty, he stood up and followed the man ahead of him out the door. The sun shone brightly on the tarmac, and the air smelled of the outdoors and green things—nearly pure, except for the jet fuel.

The clique of passengers waited beside the plane as the

pilot and a mechanic wearing overalls accessed the luggage compartment, and began stacking bags on the apron of the airstrip. After the passengers located their bags, they headed into the terminal building.

Kevin found his two bags rather quickly: one small, to carry over his shoulder, and a larger one on wheels. Then he too made his way inside, which he immediately observed was noticeably lacking in the buzz and bustle of a New York transportation hub and the brisk, hurried movements of a city crowd. For one thing, no one seemed in a hurry or cared about what time it was. Their main concerns apparently revolved around being reunited with their loved ones, and catching up on the details of each other's lives. Kevin watched them for a while, thinking that this was life outside of the city. The newness and lack of familiarity stung him keenly; the spacious interior and the absence of crowds were as foreign to him as another country would be.

He scanned the area, looking for someone. And then he saw her—tall and lean with long brunette hair and big blue eyes—his cousin, Linda Whitehouse. She wore skinny-legged jeans and a tank top without a bra. She displayed all the exuberance of youth in the thrill of discovery that her body was growing attractive to men. Kevin thought of the process as a kind of seasonal change for a young woman. He pondered for an instant what made her suddenly go boy crazy. Was it because of the media bombardment that targeted adolescents? Or was it simply a matter of hormones?

On seeing Linda again, Kevin was reminded of the last time he made the mistake of coming up to Brandon for a family visit—a visit everyone resented but felt compelled to attend lest they be accused of snubbing a relative. Then, after the first twenty minutes, the bloodletting began in its usual fashion. Maybe, he thought, this time would be different.

As Kevin approached his cousin, he saw that her tank top was actually borderline indecent, with her breasts partially exposed at the wide-open sides. Didn't her parents see her when she stepped out of the house this morning? Did she enjoy provoking them by wearing such revealing clothes?

"Where's your shirt, Linda?" Kevin asked, trying to suppress the real level of exasperation he felt.

"What do you mean? I'm wearing it," she said matter-of-factly as she tugged the fabric at the sides of her top. "Look at you, Kev"— a friendly punch to the shoulder—"a big-time police detective in New York City. You must be some hotshot, huh?"

"Where are you parked?" Kevin asked, abruptly changing the subject.

"Is that all you got?" she asked, referring to his bags.

"Yeah, this is it."

"Well, let's get moving then!" She reached up and grabbed the strap of his bag to free it from his shoulder and sling it across her own.

Together they made their way through the small terminal, past the café and bagel place, the car rental counter and newsstand, out the front doors to the parking lot.

"So, how are things with you?" Linda asked.

"Not bad, considering the fact that my father just died a few days ago," Kevin said as he walked across the lot, greedily inhaling the fresh country air.

"Do you have anyone special back in the city?"

"Yes, I do."

"That's good news... what's her name?"

"Margaret."

"Margaret, what?"

"Margaret Alexander."

"Do you like her a lot?"

"Yes, very much," he answered, hoping that would put an end to her questions.

"Why didn't she come with you?"

"It didn't feel right to bring her here for the first time, for this particular occasion," Kevin explained.

Linda fell silent as they approached her 2006 Chrysler Pacifica Limited. Once Kevin was comfortably settled in the passenger seat, she pulled out of the space and headed off to the main road.

"Were there any new findings connected to Dad's death?" Kevin asked.

"Well, since the garage was packed with explosives— what Uncle Richard called his Tonka toys—everyone pretty much agrees that the explosion that killed him was an accident."

Kevin thought about that as he looked out at the greenery surrounding them, the tall trees basking in the afternoon sun, stirring and swaying in the breeze. "In my world, that's unheard of. Dad never played with explosives as if they were toys. He was an expert in defusing bombs. He was a demolitions expert in the military, for chrissakes."

"Well, the police found no evidence of foul play, Kevin. Their report states that he was in the garage making more and more complex devices to defuse, and one just got the better of him. I mean, c'mon, he wasn't out there making ice cream."

"Does that sound reasonable to you?"

"I don't know *what* sounds reasonable, Kev. All I know is that there was the earsplitting, earth-shattering explosion that lifted your father's garage into the air like toothpicks, and almost knocked your house over. *If* there was a suicide note in the room with him, it's probably burned up, too messed up to read—or even find in the next town over," she added.

"It still doesn't sound like my father—the person I knew him to be, anyway."

"So you think he was murdered?" Linda asked, sounding dubious.

"I wouldn't put it past these people out here." Kevin got a glimpse of small ranch houses peeking through the dense foliage at intervals, their well-groomed lawns stretched out before them. There were other types too, stationary trailer homes, with cars parked on the untended yards nearby. A moment passed before he asked, "Who's leading the investigation?"

"Carville, the chief of police."

"Carville? He's *still* the police chief here?" Kevin said, nonplussed.

"Nobody else wants the job," she said, only half-joking.

"I could see that. How about his deputy? Is it still Clarke?"

"Yeah, Clarke Peppard. They're the odd couple of Brandon, Vermont," Linda said with a smirk.

"If it's not an imposition, would you mind taking me straight to the police station?"

"What for? You just got here, and Dad and Paul are dying to see you."

"I need to get a copy of the accident report as soon as possible."

"Are you kidding me?" But when Linda saw the determined look on Kevin's face, she gave a resigned sigh as she made a sweeping right onto Route 7 North towards Rutland, and Brandon beyond.

The precinct was housed in a wide, red brick building surrounded by trees and shrubs. Linda drove into the parking lot on the right side of the structure and took the first available space.

Kevin quickly slid out of the car, saying, "I won't be long." He went around the side to make his way to the entrance. Once inside, he walked past a small, empty waiting room, until he came to a desk shielded by a white picket balustrade. Behind the desk sat a dark-haired woman of indeterminate age, wearing horn-rimmed glasses over sad, tired eyes.

"Can I help you?" she asked, addressing Kevin.

"Yes, I hope you can." Instinctively, he tried to move closer so he wouldn't have to speak loudly, but the barrier stopped him. "I need to speak to either the M.E. on the Whitehouse case, or the lead investigator."

The receptionist smirked. "Lead investigator? You mean police chief Carville?"

"Uh… I guess him then."

"Wait a moment, please."

Kevin turned away from her and started pacing, glancing

around as he did at the deserted room that contained just a few benches and chairs—nothing to look at except what utility dictated.

Presently, a tall, broad-shouldered man with a fresh crew cut approached from one of the offices in the back. He was dressed in a starched and pressed light blue uniform, with knee-high black boots polished to a high shine and a ten-gallon hat perched on his head. The police chief looked like a man who was tightly wrapped, yet his face had a pleasantly paternal and lantern-jawed expression.

He extended his hand to Kevin. "Labrec Carville—chief of police—pleased to meet you."

Kevin shook his hand. "Pleased to meet you too, Chief. My name is Kevin Whitehouse, Richard Whitehouse's son."

"Oh, so you're the boy?"

"Yeah, his son."

"Well, shit my pants!" Carville exclaimed with a grin. "You are that *high-powered* detective from New York, aren't you?"

"Well, I was," Kevin admitted.

"What happened? You got burned out?"

"Something like that."

"So what brings you here?" he asked, beginning to sound cautious.

"I and a colleague of mine who's also a private investigator would like to review the police report regarding my father's death."

"I don't know if I can do that, son. You aren't police and you're not of this jurisdiction."

"We'll also need to see the medical examiner's report."

"That might be hard to do, too. You see, we don't have a medical examiner here. We have to ship the bodies down to Rutland to get their M.E. to do the work for us."

"Did you have a C.S.I. team go over the crime scene?"

Nodding his head in the affirmative, Carville added, "Also from Rutland."

"Well, they must have their reports in by now. We just want to look them over."

"I know what you want to do, son." Carville rocked back and forth on his heels. "You want to hold the lil' ol' police chief's hand and make certain that he is doing the best job that he can for your dead father. Well, guess what? I'm doing just that."

"Sir, this is my *father* we're talking about. I want to personally review the circumstances of his death," Kevin said, almost imploringly, "not tell you how to do your job. Maybe we can even be of some use to you in the investigation. I promise, we won't get in the way."

"Well, I don't need any help right now, Kevin. As you can see, this isn't New York, and we don't have murders marching through the door every hour on the hour," Carville shot back, on the defensive now.

The conversation was suddenly interrupted by the receptionist, who called out to Carville, "Sir, I have Deputy Peppard on the two-way. He says that Trip Hepner was murdered last night in his office."

"Glitter-Gun?" Carville replied.

"Yes, sir."

Carville stood silent for a moment, gritted his teeth, and then turned to the dispatcher, who was sitting nearby. "Go ahead and call Rutland. We'll need a team over there to process the crime scene."

"Sir," Kevin asked, "what about my father's case?"

"I'll see what I can do, but first let's do this the right way. Give me your supervisor's phone number, and I'll contact him to discuss the matter."

"Well, he isn't exactly my supervisor; I'm like a private contractor for him."

Carville hunched his shoulders. "Whatever."

Kevin went through his wallet, quickly produced Captain Jefferies' business card and handed it to Carville, who pocketed it immediately.

"His name is Captain Sam Jefferies. Please request the approval both for me and my colleague, David Allerton."

"Yeah, sure," Carville said, stepping toward an exit door and pushing it open with one hand as he added, "You just heard I have a fresh murder to investigate. So I'll have to deal with you and your issues later, Mr. Whitehouse."

Kevin slid back inside the Chrysler Pacifica and slammed the door shut.

"Wasn't much help, was he," Linda said, leaning forward and turning on the ignition.

"Not much at all. First he's not busy enough, and then he's too busy."

"Typical small-town attitude, Kev..." She backed up the car and pulled out of the lot.

"Can you drop me at my motel?"

"What about the family?" This time Linda sounded indignant.

"I'll see them later on for dinner. I just want to settle into my room first."

"You're saving the best for last, I suppose," Linda said, the irony in her voice all too apparent.

"Something like that."

Kevin hustled though the door of the motel room and wheeled his bag over to the chest of drawers. Then he grabbed the other one from Linda and dropped it on the floor in a corner of the room.

"Why don't you stay at our place?" she asked.

"I need to get some work done here, without any distractions."

She nodded, looking around the room. "This doesn't seem like such a bad place."

It was then that Kevin heard it—running water. All his senses went on high alert as he moved past Linda toward the bathroom. He swung the door open, and took a peek inside. The shower curtain was drawn and the water was indeed running. A dark figure could be seen moving around behind the translucent curtain. It suddenly stopped scrubbing its body to pull back the curtain.

The nearly bald head and African-American features of David Allerton peered at him mischievously from the opening. "Hey! Wassup? Just getting cleaned up from the long trip," he said, grinning broadly.

"I see that."

"What's going on?" Linda's voice came from the front room.

"Just checking the bathroom," Kevin said over his shoulder.

David slid the shower curtain back in place and continued to lather up vigorously. Kevin stepped outside and closed the door—pressing his back against it as Linda approached him.

"How was it?" she asked innocently.

"It's alright—pretty large for a motel. I like to check it out first, because if I don't like the bathroom, I don't take the room," he explained as he escorted her back to the front door.

"Oh, I can understand that," Linda said. "Well, I'll let you unpack and whatever… and I'll be back in about an hour to pick you up for dinner, okay?"

"Make that two."

"Okay—and take care, Kev." Linda blew him a kiss and shut the door behind her.

The second it closed, David emerged from the bathroom stark naked, energetically rubbing his head with a towel. His body was hard muscled and riddled with the scars he'd acquired fighting the unsung wars of this country. His hands had spilled a lot of blood, and he'd seen many people die. Yet he was never one to regale people with the story of his life or discuss these dark details. At the same time, he was the type of man who women swooned over when he turned on the charm—despite the perceptible aura of sadness about him.

Although David's wartime experiences made him cynical and bitter sometimes, Kevin could excuse all that. He had "credit" with Kevin; and, in fact, there was no person closer to him than David was, no one who knew him like

David did. He was more than just a friend and colleague, he was like a brother.

David headed over to the closet, his ample penis swaying from side to side as he moved. He'd already unpacked and hung up his clothes, and was now retrieving a white shirt and dark jacket.

Hearing the sound of running water again, Kevin frowned. "David, I think you left the water on."

"I did?" David answered absentmindedly, as he continued to dig through the closet, this time looking for a pair of pants.

Kevin walked past him into the bathroom and turned off the water, getting his shirt-sleeve wet in the process. When he came back to the front room, he found David getting dressed. "What do you plan on doing while I'm having dinner with my family?"

"We need a car to get around in this one-horse town," David said smugly.

"You're getting us a car?"

"Yeah, one of those cheap rental cars that goes for twenty dollars a week."

"You know, they've got a pretty good car service here in Brandon and all you have to do is dial up," Kevin suggested.

"Brandon." David laughed, ignoring Kevin's suggestion. "What kind of name is Brandon, anyway?"

"A certain statesman named Stephen A. Douglas, who was born in Brandon in 1847, came back to it later on in his life to tell the townsfolk that Brandon was a good place to be born and a good place to leave."

They both chuckled over the anecdote, despite the fact

that it had nothing to do with David's question about the name.

"You know," Kevin said thoughtfully, "we could accomplish a lot together tonight. Maybe it would be a good idea if I go along with you instead."

David was stepping into his slacks. "Sounds like you want to miss the family get-together."

"As you know, I'm not too keen on my family. It was them—and their narrow-mindedness—that made me want to leave this town."

"Well, my plan is to get the coroner's report right after I pick up the car."

"I don't think you can do that. From what I found out, you may have to wait until tomorrow morning to get your hands on it."

"Why's that?"

"Because Brandon doesn't have a medical examiner. They have to take their bodies down to Rutland where they handle their forensics."

"No kidding?"

"No kidding. Not only that, we have to wait for Police Chief Carville to get Jefferies' approval before they'll give us access to the police and forensic reports."

"Oh, I see," was David's resigned reply.

Kevin walked over to the bed and plopped down on the edge. "Anyway, I'll go with you to get the car. By that time Linda will be here to pick me up, so I can have some quiet time with my family. We'll pursue the case tomorrow."

David donned his jacket and straightened the collar.

"Quiet time with your family—" he ruminated over the phrase. "Why does that sound so unappealing?"

"Largely, because it is," Kevin said. "I'm looking forward to it like I look forward to getting my teeth pulled."

"Aha!" David exclaimed suddenly as he stepped between the beds and discovered his shoes and socks on the floor. Finding himself near the phone on the nightstand, he snatched up the receiver impulsively and dialed information for a car service. "Did you discover anything new yet about what happened to your dad?"

"Nothing other than the fact that he blew himself up."

"Blew himself up—it just doesn't make sense! What was he doing? Growing claymores in his backyard?"

"Well, you know he was in the army, E.O.D.—Explosive Ordnance Disposal, all that kind of stuff. He was a specialist, the cream of the crop in disarming live ordinance. But for practice, in his spare time, he made bombs. He built them, then disarmed them, built them, then disarmed them. It was an insane race for him. Make a bomb that can't be disarmed, then disarm it. Make a better bomb, disarm it, and so on and so forth."

David ordered the car and hung up the phone. "So he finally built the better mousetrap and got himself killed."

"Well, that's the going hypothesis."

"Are you going to the crime scene tonight, too? I mean after dinner, of course," David asked, sitting down on one of the beds to put on his socks and shoes.

"I don't know when I'll be able to politely depart the evening's amenities…"

"Alright, I'll try to do that for you—if I can get in there."

David smiled at his friend, rested his hands on his thighs and inhaled deeply. "You know how I like to roll," he added somewhat cryptically.

They climbed into the taxi, which took them to the nearby Avis storefront. David had no cash in his wallet, so Kevin had to pay for the rental with his credit card.

As they walked together out to the lot, Kevin stopped and pointed. "Great. It's over there."

David took the wheel of their new Chevrolet Aveo compact sedan, while Kevin slipped into the passenger seat.

"You'd better hurry up and get me back to the hotel before you end up meeting my family," Kevin said.

"Yeah, and if I do, you can say I'm your big, black gay lover," David chuckled.

"That's not funny. They'd never appreciate humor like that."

David dropped Kevin off in front of their motel and headed down Franklin Street, which was actually Route 7 South. It was a two-lane road bordered by dense shrubs and trees that looked like black walls of leaves in the darkness. He hung hard on the accelerator since the medical examiner's office could close at any hour down here, unless it was busier than usual because of the Whitehouse autopsy. If that were the case, there might be someone burning the midnight oil, even in a backwater town like Rutland. Despite Kevin's admonition about official sanction from Jefferies, David decided it was worth a try—he was determined to push through any obstacles in his path. But he didn't tell Kevin any of that, since he didn't want him to interfere or insist on going along—neglecting his family obligations in the process.

David was beginning to think of Richard Whitehouse's demise as a tragic and foolish mistake made by a man playing with very dangerous toys. But not wanting to speculate further on the whys and wherefores without the benefit of any facts, he reached over and turned on the radio. After flipping through several stations of music and talk, he found a local twenty-four hour news station and sat back, listening intently for any information about the accident.

Police chief carville strode into his precinct and through the waiting room on the other side of the double doors, shooing away the townsfolk who crowded around him. The news of Trip Hepner's murder had them worried and anxious for answers, but he had nothing yet to share with them. He continued on doggedly past the receptionist's desk to his office in the back. He was on edge. In addition to the two recent deaths, he had two intruders in his quiet little town; and like germs floating in the bloodstream, they triggered his emotional immune system, firing up every single one of his nerves.

The youthful looking deputy, Clarke Peppard, followed right in after him. "You've got a lot of worried people out there, Chief."

"So I noticed."

"There are also those FBI agents, Wells and Brooks, waiting for you," Peppard added, almost as an afterthought.

"Send them in and handle as many of the locals as you can."

"Sure thing," Peppard said as he left the room, returning with the two agents in tow moments later.

The two men, flanking the doorway, were neatly dressed in nearly identical comfortable-looking, dark suits. Wells stepped forward first, extending his hand, "Labrec, nice to see you again. How have you been doing?"

Carville stood and grasped his hand, "I'm doing great, Sherman. It's good to see you again too," and then added, "you too, Vincent." when he turned to look at Brooks.

"Please, please, take a seat," Carville motioned to the sofa on his right.

The two men settled themselves comfortably before Wells got down to the subject at hand. "Labrec, we're here because of the recent death of one of our colleagues," he said as he removed a pair of dark glasses from his face, folded them and stuck them carefully into the top pocket of his jacket.

"Yes, Richard Whitehouse—he died under unusual circumstances," Carville replied.

"Why unusual?"

Carville moved around some papers on his desk until he found a copy of the police report and held it out, without comment and without getting up from his desk.

Since Agent Brooks was seated closer, he stood up to retrieve the document from Carville. Brooks had longish light brunette hair, and sported a short well-trimmed beard and mustache. He wore wire-rimmed sunglasses, which, unlike his colleague, he did not remove.

"Whitehouse was a very good man," Wells remarked, while Brooks looked over the report. Wells, having darker hair, was older than Brooks by a few years, his features clean shaven and narrow. He seemed, as did Wells, too handsome to be an FBI agent.

"You wouldn't happen to have any idea about who'd do this to him? Maybe someone he helped put in jail or something like that, someone who wanted revenge?" Carville asked.

Wells shook his head to indicate a negative. "Whitehouse's examination of evidence *helped* put five men in prison, but there was always more damning evidence in play. His was just the icing on the cake. Besides, everyone he helped convict is doing hard time. When they're finally out, they'll need strollers."

Carville nodded. "Let me ask you something else...Do you know anything about these two New York cops, uh... Kevin Whitehouse—Richard's son—and David Allerton?"

Both agents looked thoughtful for a minute, until Wells said, "Never heard of them," looking to his colleague for affirmation. Brooks nodded his agreement. "How do they figure in this?" Wells added.

"They want in on the investigation. In fact, Richard's son is asking for all of the reports on the case. He's already on this like white on rice."

Brooks asked, "You have a problem with that?"

"I don't know these men," Carville said.

"Check out their records from their commanding officer," Wells suggested.

Carville reached into his jacket and produced the card that Kevin had given him. "Hmmm... *Captain* Sam Jefferies," Carville muttered, "One Police Plaza."

"Doesn't sound like a lightweight, that's for certain," Wells remarked.

Brooks focused their attention on the police report, which he'd just finished reviewing. "It says there was no suicide note left at the scene."

"So?" Wells asked him. "What does the report say—did it *look* like a suicide?"

"To me, it looks intentional, even though the report doesn't reach that conclusion. If it wasn't a suicide, then it was a murder. It definitely wasn't an accident," Brooks said with conviction.

"What makes you say that?" Wells asked.

"If he was working on an incendiary device in his garage, why was evidence of active shaped charges found at the scene?" Brooks said, pointing to the report.

"Let me see that when you're done with it," Wells said, and then, turning to Carville, added, "So, what do you plan to do about these guys from New York?"

"Call Jefferies." Carville held up the card again and reached for his phone.

Franklin clinton strolled into Captain Sam Jefferies office with a resolute air. He was a robust black man, with dark eyes, an ample nose and the beginnings of a receding hairline. Dressed in a well-pressed suit, white shirt and tie, he looked more like some Wall Street wheeler-dealer than a detective.

Jefferies' office was strictly a utilitarian affair. It was furnished with filing cabinets, a long table along one wall accessorized with organizers for forms and files, and a leather couch opposite. His desk was nearly empty save for a blotter, a telephone, a Rolodex, and some pens. There were two chairs neatly arranged in front of it.

Clinton set down two glasses on Jefferies' desk, and then began unscrewing a bottle of Gentleman Jack.

"Oh, so you're the bartender tonight?" Jefferies remarked, watching his friend remove the cap with a flourish and fill their glasses. Jefferies eyes looked tired, a five o'clock shadow revealed that he hadn't gone home in a while to shave, and his wavy hair was somewhat mussed. This appearance of his was so common of late that is was becoming his signature look.

"For everything that ails you," Clinton said, resting the bottle down and lifting his glass for a toast. "Another day behind us."

"For everything that ails you," Jefferies repeated, as he picked up his drink and knocked it back in sync with Clinton.

"You know," Clinton said as he sat and prepared to pour two more drinks. "It's a very good day when there are no new unsolved cases outstanding. In fact, that's gotta be some kind of record for this city."

Jefferies laughed. He picked up his glass and was lifting it to his lips when his phone rang. He stopped in mid-motion.

"Did you jinx me, Franklin?" Jefferies set his drink down and lifted the receiver to his ear. "Captain Sam Jefferies."

"Captain Jeffries, this is Police Chief Labrec Carville of the Brandon, Vermont police department. I'd appreciate a few moments of your time, please."

"Okay, Carville—what's going on up there in Vermont?"

"I'm dealing with a suspicious death, and the victim's son wants to be part of the investigation."

"That sounds like a dangerous proposition," Jefferies said. "But how do I figure in this?"

"The victim's name is Richard Whitehouse. His son Kevin is up here wanting access to confidential reports pertaining to the case, and he gave me your card. He said you'd vouch for him and his partner, David Allerton. That's why I'm calling."

"They are both fine men, officially out on disability for the moment. They're very good at what they do, and they'll bust your case wide open if you give them the chance."

"They're *that* good, huh?" Carville said, sounding skeptical.

Jefferies repeated, with a hint of sarcasm, "Yes, they're *that* good."

"Well, sir, I don't want them running amok in my town. If they can't play by my rules, I'll send them packing."

"You make it sound as if your rules run counter to the law," Jefferies said.

There was a pause on Carville's end. "I'm not saying that at all. I'm saying that just because I'm not a high-and-mighty cop from New York doesn't mean I'm stupid."

"They will never treat you that way—you have my word on it. I can assure you that these are good men. You can trust them."

Carville ruminated for a few beats. "Okay, on your say-so I'll give them a chance and see how it goes. Thanks, I appreciate your input."

"You're very welcome." Jefferies hung up the phone

and, practically in the same motion, picked up his glass. He drained the contents quickly, and holding it out to Clinton said, "Hey, fill me up again here."

"What was that all about?" he asked as he obliged his friend and poured him another.

"Whitehouse and Allerton."

"Oh, jeez," Clinton said with a sigh.

"Kevin's father died. Since I don't know how fucked-up this can make him, I better consult his doctor right way," Jefferies said, reaching for his Rolodex.

THE DINNER PARTY

Some get-together, Kevin thought as he strode into his uncle's modest ranch house. His father never really got along with his brother—his Uncle Nick—except when they joined forces against a common foe. Then they were a team to be reckoned with. But once the problem was resolved, they'd be adversaries again.

The bad feelings probably stemmed from the days of their earliest youth, when they competed unsuccessfully for their father's affections. Since neither one received it, they turned their disappointment and bitterness on each other. Their father, Richard Whitehouse Sr., was a dour and serious man who treated his sons like soldiers, not children. Consequently, the family languished in a joyless, unloving environment whenever their father was around. Their mother tried as she might to bring a sense of love and caring to the young men, but she was constantly eclipsed by the towering laborer that would appear home at the end of the day. He would darken the doorway, and darken the home with his despite. So much so that the young men could feel it like a third parent in the house, a dark force that was a source of disapproval for them.

To Kevin, Richard Whitehouse Sr. was the perfect model for his father, Richard Jr.

Uncle Nick stood in the threshold of the front door to welcome Kevin, extending a hand that his nephew shook vigorously. Kevin searched his face for signs of his father in his features, but the brothers never bore much of a resemblance to each other. Nick was tall and lanky, with sandy-colored hair that was always neatly parted to one side. His deep frown lines had started forming in adolescence. He wore wire-rimmed glasses that had a habit of sliding down the bridge of his nose.

"Good to see you, Kevin. I just wish it was under better circumstances," he said, his voice sounding sorrowful and constricted.

"It's good to see you again too, Uncle Nick."

His uncle stepped aside to let Kevin and Linda enter.

When she came to pick him up at his motel, Kevin was relieved to see that she'd changed her clothes. Wearing a sensible skirt and blouse, she was far more presentably attired than she'd been that morning.

Once inside, his aunt Charity rushed over to greet him; she was an older blonde replica of her daughter, with a figure still youthful and curvaceous. She was wearing an apron over her sweater and slacks.

"Kevin! Is that you?" she exclaimed, then rushed into his arms, hugging him tightly. "Oh, my dear boy, why did you stay away from us for so long?"

Kevin, still wrapped in her embrace and suppressing a groan, replied, "Just work, Aunt Charity."

She released him from her stranglehold, and took a step back to look him up and down. "My, what a handsome young man! Come on in and sit down!" She waved him into the living room, where he sat down on the slipcovered couch.

His uncle was already seated on a straight-backed chair across from him, while his cousin Paul, silent up to now, stationed himself on an ottoman by the fireplace. Charity and Linda vanished down a corridor that led deeper into the house.

"I know you and your father didn't see eye to eye on many things, Kevin, but he was still a good man," he said as if pursuing a dialogue already in progress.

"How was he during the last days when you saw him, Uncle Nick?"

"Okay, but maybe a little more withdrawn than usual. As a rule, he didn't come to many of the family cookouts and get-togethers, so it was hard to tell. He was a solitary man who loved to tinker around in that garage of his. I always thought about him up there. Once I went to talk to him about not making the family parties and he barked at me. He had a hard edge to him that was pretty fierce. Him being from the military and all. He could be very caustic."

"I can actually believe that, Uncle Nick. He had a very short temper that we even never crossed. Living with him was like walking on eggshells. Let me ask you, do you mean the extension on the house?"

"Yeah, the extension on the house," Nicholas sat back and made large gestures with his hands, making a rectangular form. "He used to always call it his barn or his workshop," Nicholas nodded.

"Yeah, I used to keep him company there sometimes," Paul suddenly chimed in. Not long out of high school, he was tall and lean like his sister, his body just turning into that of a man's. A few pimples marked his features, his eyes were bright and shiny. He seemed to revel in the memories of his eccentric uncle, either that or he was amazed at his abilities. "He kept all these interesting tools and devices that he liked to experiment with. And anything could blow up at any time—if he let it."

"He actually detonated some of those devices?" Kevin asked, nonplussed.

Nick turned to address his son. "You never told me anything like that," he said, sounding irate.

Paul looked uncomfortable now, pushing a shock of long hair from before his eyes. "Just the little ones, with a little charge. They went pop, like firecrackers, nothing really big. He would take them out to the backyard on some days and I would watch."

"I wonder if one of his 'pop toys' caught up with him," Nick mumbled as he shifted around to face Kevin again.

"Maybe it did," Kevin remarked.

"Are you planning to investigate your father's accident?"

"You can call it an accident, Uncle Nick. But from what I know so far, this could be a murder until proven otherwise."

His uncle simply nodded his understanding.

Kevin pulled a small, palm-sized IC recorder from his jacket pocket and turned it on. "In fact, I'd like to ask you a few questions, Uncle Nick."

"Am *I* being recorded?"

"Yes."

"I don't think I like that idea," he said flatly.

"Well, this way I get your statement verbatim, which is

more accurate than jotting down what I think you said and meant."

"Like I already said, I don't think I want to make a statement, Kevin," his uncle said, sounding more emphatic this time.

"Don't you want to help me, Uncle Nick? My father—your brother—might have been killed by someone who thinks they can get away with murder. If this was something other than an accident, I have to catch the perpetrator—and getting a statement from you is a good start."

His uncle gave a sigh of resignation and signaled Kevin to go ahead.

"This is Kevin Whitehouse speaking. With me are Nicholas Whitehouse and his son Paul." Addressing his uncle, he asked, "Did you see anyone or anything suspicious near Richard Whitehouse's home in the days preceding his death?"

Nick thought about the question long and hard. "No, I can't say that I did. I wasn't up there much at all. He lives all the way up Route 7, off the Steinberg Road turnoff, where it's about as deserted as you can get. C'mon, Kevin, you know he liked his privacy."

"Yeah, I know about that. His privacy was hard to deal with even when we were growing up," Kevin agreed. "How about you, Paul?" Kevin turned to his cousin.

Paul shook his head. "It was always just him and me up there. I never saw him with anyone else."

Kevin, returning to Nick, asked: "Do you know of anyone who would have wanted him hurt or killed?"

"Nope, not that I can think of. He spent a lot of his time with the Feds. Rich was not someone easily understood—he was a loner and kept to himself. Not much of a conversationalist or a friend, either. I can tell you, he didn't like people much, and he wasn't one of those types that you want to be a close friend with. I loved my brother, don't get me wrong, but he was a son-of-a-gun when we were growing up. Always getting into fights, always a turd kicker. You had to cut him some slack to understand him. Your father was a little off, a little messed up in the head."

Kevin nodded, because he was only too familiar with his uncle's description of his father. His father was a cold fish, like a portion of his soul was missing. Kevin turned to Paul, who shook his head.

"Paul, can you speak up so that I can get it on the recording?"

"No," he replied. "No one. He didn't seem to have any enemies...or friends. But Pop is right, he did have a nasty temper and really didn't care about people. He didn't mind me though. I think he liked me."

Kevin nodded again, pensively. "Uncle Nick, can you tell me what you were doing the night that he was killed?"

"Hmmm," he thought about that for a second. "I was right here. I had a couple of beers and then watched *King of the Hill* reruns before going to sleep."

"I guess Aunt Charity can vouch for that, right?"

"Yes, she was here too."

"How about you, Paul?"

Paul looked nervous as soon as the question was directed at him. "I was out with some friends of mine at the bowling alley. We were there almost all night."

"I'm certain that you have a lot of witnesses to that."

"Sure, I can give you their names."

"Not necessary."

Kevin punched the button on his IC recorder and stashed it back into his jacket. "Well, I think that's it for now. Sorry for the intrusion."

"Well, I guess once a cop, always a cop, right, Kevin?" his uncle said fondly, relieved that the interview was over.

"Dinner's ready," Linda called out from the dining room.

Kevin stood and followed his uncle and cousin into the modest dining room and took the seat offered him at the head of the table. He looked around at the walls as the food was being served. They were adorned mostly with framed photographs and lithographs of covered bridges and rustic views of the Vermont landscape, interspersed here and there with family pictures. He peered at them intently, but couldn't make out the finer details from where he sat.

"Let us now say grace," Charity announced from the far end of the table, reaching out to take hold of her husband's hand on her left and Linda's on her right, which caused them all to reach for the hand of the person sitting next to them until they made an unbroken circle.

Nick followed with a quick, simple prayer for "the boys" overseas, the good men behind bars, those trying to feed their families, and for his own. After that, everyone began eating.

In a brief pause between the scraping sounds of silverware on plates, Nick turned to Kevin. "How have you been doing since your accident? Are you still experiencing any side effects?"

Kevin stopped eating, looking up from his fork. "I was, but I'm doing better now."

"Do you mind telling us what happened?"

Kevin swallowed hard and dodged the question. "It happened quite a while ago."

"I heard you went on disability. But for what?" his uncle persisted.

"At first it was physical, but now it's a mental condition."

"That's from the accident, too?"

"Kind of," Kevin said evasively.

Charity leaned across the table, her voice consoling. "Is there anything we can do to help you, Kevin? After all, you *are* family."

"I know," he nodded. "I know."

"So what do you do with your time now?" Linda asked, considerately changing the subject.

"I investigate criminal cases—especially those that others find too gnarly to deal with."

"Do you do this alone?" his uncle asked, refraining from eating while he looked at Kevin expectantly.

"No, I work with another detective. He can easily get in and out of some pretty sticky situations, so he gathers up evidence that can sometimes be harder for me to get."

"Why is that?" Paul looked puzzled.

"Well, he's good in the field. He has army training and knows all this martial arts stuff. He's just better at some things than I am."

Obviously feeling sated, Nick leaned back with a sigh. "He sounds like an interesting guy. Is he here in Brandon with you?"

"Yeah. In fact, he's already working on some of the preliminaries for the investigation into Dad's death."

"In that case, why don't you bring him over to say hello while you're both here," his uncle suggested.

Suddenly, Charity perked up. "Yes, Kevin—you should bring him over."

"I don't really think he'd be too comfortable with a visit. He's not really a people person. He keeps to himself most of the time." Kevin glanced up briefly to read their faces, then looked down at his plate again.

"Poor man. Did something happen to him, too?" Aunt Charity asked.

"Is he on disability, too?" Nick added, with evident concern.

"Yes."

"Same reasons?"

"Yeah, pretty much."

"Sounds like you two guys have a lot in common."

"That's very true, Uncle Nick."

"You've got to be kidding me. Do you know what fucking time it is? It's after eleven." The skinny college kid stood at the door facing down David Allerton, who was illuminated only by the entryway light.

Behind him night had fallen, and the tall trees that lined the dark deserted path sighed as their branches rustled in the night's breeze. David looked up at the large granite building and then at the kid, and wondered if his trip was in vain. Then he reached calmly into his jacket pocket and produced his badge. "I'm a private investigator working on this case. Can you cut me some slack?"

"Why? Where are you from?"

"New York City. I'm here to investigate the recent accident."

The kid frowned, looking over the top of his wire rimmed glasses. "You mean Richard Whitehouse's accident?"

David nodded. "His son is a close friend of mine, and we're trying to determine whether his death was the result of foul play."

"New York? You have no jurisdiction in Vermont," the young technician pointed out.

"C'mon, consider it a professional courtesy."

The kid thought about it, looked behind him, then back to David. He stepped away and swung the door open, allowing him in. "What exactly do you want at this time of night?"

David stepped inside, scratched the side of his smooth jaw and looked around the spartan foyer. "Could I see the victim's remains—and the reports?"

"Follow me," the kid said. He turned and left with David right behind him.

The rooms and corridors of the medical examiner's office looked surprisingly like a hospital: there were nurses sauntering by, as well as doctors moving from room to room. The kid, dressed in a long, white lab coat, led David down a corridor that did not descend into a sub-ground floor like so many of the other morgues he was familiar with. This one opened into a large main room that was aboveground, with broad high windows that probably provided ample illumination during the day, but now glowed only dimly with moonlight. The kid flicked a switch near the door, awakening dome lights that spread pools of white around them as they crossed an area filled with examination and instrument tables, head blocks, and empty body trays.

The kid went over to a cadaver drawer, checked the name on the label, and tugged on a handle that allowed it to slide out smoothly. He stopped short of pulling it out all the way. In the middle of the tray was a metal container covered with a sheet.

"Are you ready for this?" the kid asked David.

David reached for the sheet on his own and pulled it aside, revealing the parts of a man. There was a charred head, broken and empty, the scorched face tattered. The eyes were missing, as were the lips, while the few remaining teeth formed a tight obscene grin. There were also humerus and radial bones of the left arm, as well as a badly burned right foot, a fibula from the calf, and four metacarpal bones from one of the hands.

"Is this it? Was there enough tissue left to do a toxicology report?" David asked.

"There was. He was clean. Nothing odd in the blood-stream except alcohol," the kid replied.

"Do you know what blew him up?"

"I was told it was something he made himself. I don't know what he was working on, and no one wanted to enter what was left of his shop until after the people from E.O.D. made sure there were no other bombs lying around. What I do know is that the device packed enough punch to rip his garage apart—it contained around ten to fifteen sticks of dynamite. Still, that's just what I heard. You'll have to talk to the demolition boys to get more accurate information."

David nodded. "Thanks, I'll do that."

The kid replaced the sheet, slid the draw back, and

crossed the room to a desk scattered with file folders. "I have a copy of the report right here."

"Great," David said as he lagged behind the kid, stopping to look at the faces of the otherwise covered corpses that were lined up in neat rows. He noticed that two of them were training dummies, the skin of their faces plastic and lifeless. The next one was probably a mature man, but it was very hard to tell. The face had been badly smashed and was distorted—pulpy and covered in heavy streaks of blood. David paused to pull the sheet back further from the body, revealing extensive bruises and abrasions on the chest area and forearms.

"What happened here?" David asked. "A car accident?"

As the kid picked up the folder for the Whitehouse examination, he looked up to see what David was referring to. "Oh, that's Trip Hepner. He's been Brandon's town jeweler for almost twenty years. It looks like someone took a heavy instrument and beat him to death with it."

"Was any jewelry stolen from his store?" David asked.

"Not that I know of. I just get the bodies, you know."

David pointed to the folder in the kid's hand. "Is that for me?"

"Oh, yeah," he said as he handed it over to David, who took it and immediately began flipping through the photographs and reports. But then he stopped abruptly and after a thoughtful pause, nodded toward Hepner's corpse. "What about this guy? How's his report coming along?"

"We'll know more about him tomorrow."

David reached into his jacket for his wallet, retrieving a hundred-dollar bill that he handed to the kid. "There's a lot more where that came from."

"Hey, thanks." The kid pocketed the cash.

"What's your name, by the way?"

"John Paulin."

David paused, looking the kid up and down. "How come you have a full run of the place? You're not the janitor."

John laughed. "I'm the assistant M.E., or you can say the apprentice. I work closely with the M.E. and at night he tends to give me the shit work to do so that he can look like he worked all night the next morning. But I don't really care, it's a good job. I like dead bodies."

"That's pretty creepy."

"It's not actually. A body is a body."

Nodding, David slipped the file under his arm. "You live out here?"

"Yeah, in Rutland."

"Keep up the good work, John. If you don't mind, I'll probably be needing a lot more help from you."

"No problem. You got it," John smiled. "Just come at night—like you did this time—and if anyone in an official capacity asks you, don't tell them you got anything from me."

"Why, will you get into trouble?"

John hunched his shoulders. "I really don't care. Like I said, it's a good job, but the M.E. can be a real asshole at times. This is like a little dig back at him. I have skills you know, and can be a source of information, not just someone to do grunt work."

"I see." David held out his hand, shaking his. "Thank you, John."

"Like I said, don't mention it."

Nick stepped outside with his glass of iced tea to sit on a wooden bench on the darkened porch. He contemplated the full moon glowing incandescent in the night sky and the scudding clouds as they slipped past the stars. A few minutes later, Kevin came out and sat in the nearby Adirondack chair, stretching out comfortably with his iced tea. Paul, right behind him, headed over to the edge of the porch and rested a shoulder against one of its narrow white pillars, enjoying the cool evening breezes against his body.

Nick stirred the tea and ice with his finger. "Why didn't your father ever visit you in New York?"

Kevin hunched his shoulders almost defensively as he reflected on the reasons. "He didn't much like the idea of my being a cop in a crime-ridden city. He believed that New York was too dangerous, and had reached a critical point in the seventies—that it became something to escape from, not go to. He thought I was a little crazy for wanting to go to college there."

"How do you feel about it?"

"New York is New York. Either you grow a hard shell so you can handle the murders, rapes, and robberies you encounter, or you leave. It's just that simple. By now, I'm inured to it. It's my home, and just like you like it here, I like it there."

"You like it there?"

"Yeah," Kevin said as he raised the glass to his lips.

"Even after your accident?"

Kevin purposely kept on drinking so as not to reply immediately. He'd grown weary of dwelling on the accident...

the maddeningly loud screech of skidding vehicles, the screaming, dying people, the trucks rolling over like dice in a crap game, the explosions, the smells, the terrific heat. It was an unbearable assault on every one of the five senses.

Also, it seemed to him as if everyone everywhere knew about it: through colleagues or friends, or from the newspapers or TV. Of course, Kevin's family was notified when he was admitted into the ICU. Although nobody came to visit, they knew he was there and why. Despite being at a distance, their frequent phone calls made it clear they were very concerned about his well-being: Would he ever walk again? Would he regain his sight in both eyes? All the while, he himself wondered whether he would remain sane and lucid—and alive.

Kevin closed his eyes and his world blurred, just as it had done so many years ago outside of the windows of his unmarked car. Now he opened them again, only to find himself in Brandon, Vermont, bathed in a cold sweat, the glass of iced tea sliding from his hand. He moved quickly to catch it in a two-handed purchase, smiling tightly to himself.

"Whoa! Cousin Kev, are you alright there?" Paul called from the edge of the porch.

"Yes, I'm fine," Kevin nodded, regaining his composure as he wiped the icy glass across his forehead.

"I see now that the accident's not your favorite subject," Uncle Nick said. "I'm sorry I brought it up."

"No problem." Kevin shook his head, as if regretting being so close-mouthed. "It's just that I try not to think about it too much."

"Well, then—to change the subject—I wonder who

Carville will get to set off the fireworks this year, now that Rich is dead."

"Dad did that, too?"

"Yeah—heck, your old man did everything. He used to blow old stumps right out of the ground. One man, one shot. After he came along, your problems were gone."

"But didn't he knock down the Prestons' house one year, Dad?" Paul asked.

Nick pointed to his son, as he started remembering the incident. "Yeah, he did do that, didn't he?"

"A jack of all trades... huh?" Kevin asked.

"And a master of 'em all too," his uncle replied.

"Well, it's getting late," Kevin said as he rose tiredly to his feet. "It's almost nine."

Paul approached him, and took the glass from his hand. "I'll get the car to take you back to your motel, Kev."

Kevin smiled as the young man re-entered the house.

Nick got up from the bench to face his nephew. "I know that what you'll be going through in the next couple of days will be very difficult, so I just wanted to let you know that I'm here for you." He clapped a hand against Kevin's shoulder twice and steered him down the steps and onto the front lawn.

Although it was early fall, Kevin could still hear the loud chirping of the crickets.

"Again, I'm really sorry to have brought up your accident, Kevin. You've had enough of death."

Kevin's eyes were locked on the headlights of the approaching car coming around the house, with Paul at the wheel.

"Do you know when you'll be going back?"

"It's strange, Uncle Nick," Kevin said, ignoring his last question. "I faintly recollect my partner being killed in that accident, and yet I feel the same way about him as I do about my father—I don't feel a thing. I feel like what's happened is real, but somehow it just isn't substantial enough to merit any emotional response. When I think about them, I feel dead inside."

"That can't be good, can it? I mean, shouldn't you feel *something*?"

"Well, when I try too hard to generate a feeling—like sadness—I instantly feel something else. My doctor labeled it 'inappropriate emotional response'—one that doesn't fit the circumstances because I'm forcing whatever it is I do feel."

"Forcing your feelings, you mean?" his uncle asked, sympathetically.

Kevin nodded, looking down at his shoes. "I don't feel about them as I should. And coming up to Brandon, what I feel is not so much the loss of my father, but a desire to get to the bottom of how he died."

"You think someone killed him?" Nick said, trying unsuccessfully to look into his nephew's eyes.

Kevin kept his eyes averted and seemed totally dejected. "Yeah. Considering Dad's expertise in explosives, I don't believe he could have made such a huge mistake. That's why I want to see the reports and the crime scene."

"You call it a crime scene, but it might not be."

"For me it is, until it isn't," Kevin said flatly, finally meeting his uncle's gaze.

"You keep your chin up, young man. You'll get to the bottom of it," Nick said, nodding his encouragement.

"I'm going to do my damnedest. If I can't feel pain for my loss, I'll feel the satisfaction of getting to the bottom of this, crime or not."

"Good," Nick said as he patted him on the back affectionately several times, before the two headed over to the blue Chevy Malibu that was still waiting in front of the house. Paul leaned over to push open the passenger-side door.

"I'll see you at the funeral," Kevin said to his uncle before he got in.

Nick nodded. "See you there. Let me know if you need anything."

Kevin shook his head. "Thanks, but I'll be fine."

"Are you going to bring your friend?"

"Probably not. He's going to push on and do the digging for me while I'm busy."

Uncle Nick smiled. "Good luck then, son."

Kevin climbed in, and Paul pulled onto the dirt road that led from their property into the main road. He kicked on his high beams.

"What do you have planned for tomorrow, Kev?" he asked.

"I want to start investigating my dad's death, before the trail turns really cold."

"Do you think you'll need any help getting around?"

Kevin shrugged his shoulders noncommittally.

"Why don't you keep me on speed-dial, and if you need me, I'll come." He waited for Kevin to retrieve his cell phone, before reciting his number so he could program it in.

"Thanks, Paul. I'll keep your offer in mind."

"I've always had a soft spot for police work. I think I could be a pretty good cop."

Kevin turned to him and smiled. "How old are you, Paul?"

"Twenty-five."

"Well, you're certainly of age. Why don't you come down to the city and apply for the police academy?"

"Do you think they'd take me?"

"Who knows, but I'll let you in on a secret: it's a tough job."

Paul was silent for a moment, and then changed the subject. "Tell me about Uncle Richard. Was he as crazy as Mom and Pop say he was?"

"Is that what they're calling him?"

"Yeah, they were saying stuff like he was the mad bomber living in a shack up in the hills. A lot of people were saying it. He didn't even come into town much anymore."

"Unfortunately, I didn't know my father very well. He never sent me postcards or letters, and there was no weekly phone call—or even the annual Christmas dinner."

"Yeah, he never came over to our house for the holidays, either."

"I remember him as a great dad when it counted, though. I never wanted for anything. He might not have been all that attentive or sentimental, that I can remember. But he changed a lot once he was in the service. After he enlisted and began doing tours of duty, other things began to take priority: the platoon, the regiment, the job in general... everything but the family. And then when he did come home, he was standoffish, cold and elusive even after he left the military. By the time my brother Simon and I should have developed a father-son relationship with him, we were already moving apart emotionally and geographically. Simon left for parts unknown by joining the military, later I left for college and the police academy in New York."

"Hmmm… I see."

"How did he seem to you?"

Paul tilted his head slightly to look out the driver's-side window at the passing landscape, then shifted his gaze back to the windshield. "I never really knew Uncle Richard all that well, even though I spent some time with him. He hardly ever came over to our house and we never went over to his, except when the Fourth came around. He needed help then, so he would show up to ask my dad and me to give him a hand.

"That was when we saw another side of him. He was much funnier and much friendlier at those times. He would invite us up to the house and into his garage, and show us his devices and the neat tricks he could do with them. It was as if being around so many explosives was like a drug for him. I would stay up there with Uncle Richard after Pop left, and he would show me lots more. And I'd go back sometimes on my own since he seemed to like my company. I've only been in his house a couple of times, when he had some important business to take care of, but mostly it was to his garage."

There was silence for a minute as Paul considered what he wanted to say next. "I noticed you didn't want to talk to Dad about police business. Is there something you *can* talk about with me?"

In answer, Kevin cracked a wan smile that ended their conversation.

Paul dropped Kevin off in front of the motel. He pulled out of the lot and then slipped away into the night. Kevin watched him drive off, and then headed over to his room. He was surprised to see that the lights were on inside—which had to mean that David was home. When he stopped in front of the door and started fumbling for his key, a car horn honked. He looked around in the dark, but saw nothing to indicate that the sound had anything to do with him. The car horn blared again as Kevin inserted the key in the lock. This time, when he turned around, he had a better idea of the direction the sound was coming from. Off to his right, the headlights of a Chevrolet Aveo flickered on. Kevin strolled over to the vehicle, came around to lean against the driver's-side door and peered in the open window.

"Going to bed?" David asked.

"No. I was just going in to read the M.E. reports. Did you get them?"

"They're right here," David said as he tapped the narrow folder sitting on the passenger seat. "It's not much, but it's all they've got right now."

"Where are you off to?" Kevin asked.

"Your father's house."

Kevin nodded and came around to the passenger side. He grabbed the folder from the seat before he slipped into it.

"So, what have you learned?" Kevin asked.

David shifted the car into reverse, and backed out of the space. "That they don't know much."

Kevin turned on the overhead light and started thumbing through the pages. "I see that the preliminary crime scene report is here, too. The C.S.I. guys in Rutland move pretty fast. They found an evidence of an accelerant. Detonator. Devices."

David headed north up Route 7 towards Steinberg Road. "Check out page eight. They found a lot of things, like timers, digital detonators, along with shaped charges."

"What's that supposed to mean?"

"There were four shaped charges on the house side of the room, and what might have been a dispersal incendiary device in the center of the workshop. That doesn't look good for your father, Kevin."

"It looks like it was designed to bring down the garage only," Kevin replied breathlessly.

"Bring it all down, burn it all up, and then scatter the pieces by way of the secondary devices that were found. The shaped charges were meant to send those pieces flying away from the house itself, probably to protect it from the blasts and the flaming debris."

"So this is going to be pawned off as a suicide, huh?"

"It could have been an elaborate plan for one. I mean, your father did have the skills to pull off such a wild finish."

"Or someone could have tied him up in the middle of the room, set up the shaped charges, the incendiary devices and the timer, and drove a safe distance away before the fireworks started."

"That sounds kind of loony, Kev. Your father was the demolitions expert. It would take another expert of his caliber to stage something that sophisticated. "

"You mean you don't like my theory."

"That's correct."

"Son-of-a-bitch, David! My father was murdered!" Kevin barked at his partner.

"I do not doubt you, buddy, but I am going to play the police chief here and ask: where's your proof?"

"The shape charges?" Kevin looked quizzically at his partner.

"That's one of the hurdles you'll have to overcome if you want to sell murder. Why would a fucking killer care if the explosions brought down the rest of the house? Why would they care, Kevin? Only someone with a vested interest in protecting the integrity of the house would use shaped charges to do away with just the garage and its contents. Only the owner of the house would take such care."

Kevin remained silent. "My father would never have killed himself." He closed the folder and gazed out the window, contemplating the wall of trees speeding by, trying to take his mind off the thoughts buzzing around in his head like angry bees. "Call it a gut feeling, but I know my father and he wasn't the type of man to give up on anything. He was like a stone statue, indomitable, a force to be dealt with, not some weak individual that would feel so sorry for himself so as to take his own life."

David reached up to turn off the overhead light. "Do you want me to turn the car around?"

"No, I want to see the house."

In time, Steinberg Road parted into a wide fork where it was replaced by Hollow Road North and South. David turned down the north fork, and after traversing several yards he noticed a bright light illuminating the skies behind a rise in the land ahead. He parked on a shoulder of the dirt road and killed the engine. The two left the car and continued up the road on foot until it crested, where they were suddenly greeted by the sight of a large crew of men—presumably from Rutland's C.S.I. department—carefully sifting through the rubble with the aid of Caterpillar trucks, backhoes, and shovels. Flood lamps, strategically positioned around the grounds of Richard Whitehouse's home, bathed the scene in a ghostly glare amidst the otherwise dark early hours of morning.

Just as David said, Kevin could see that practically nothing was left of the garage—yet the house remained intact. There sat his childhood home of two stories, cream-colored siding, and a wide front porch braced by four columns. Further along, at the structure's rear left corner, was blown-out rubble. Studs stood naked in the dark, some shattered like broken matchsticks. A wide blast crater in the middle of where the garage had stood sprayed debris in all directions.

Kevin and David, so far unnoticed by the men—who were clearly absorbed in their work—made their way under the police tape toward the blast site. When they reached its perimeter, they started scanning the ground, which was littered with shattered glass, finely splintered wood and other debris, for clues. Everything crunched underfoot, while the acrid smell of burning still filled the air.

"We need to speak with the head investigator, please," Kevin said to one of the men, tapping him on the shoulder to gain his attention. When there was no response, Kevin repeated his request.

"He's over there. His name is Roger Kawamura and he's

with the Rutland Fire Department." The man pointed across the debris field to a solitary figure intent on his task.

Kevin and David crossed a long stretch of rubble to approach the team's leader. His Asian features were set in stern lines. The name Kawamura was sewn over the left breast pocket of his uniform. He looked very tired as he pulled himself upright to address Kevin. "Who are you? A junior G-man?"

Kevin shook his head and produced his shield. "My name is Kevin Whitehouse, and I'm a private investigator from New York. I've got a few questions for you."

Kawamura sighed. "Even if you're a relative of the deceased, aren't you way out of your jurisdiction?"

David started to snarl a reply, but Kevin cut him off. "Since the man who died in this explosion was my father, I'm hoping you could tell me if you think his death was a suicide or not—at least based on what you know so far."

Roger Kawamura looked hard into Kevin's eyes, as if trying to gauge his sincerity. "The victim was your father?"

David, satisfied now that his friend had the situation well in hand, again became preoccupied with the debris field. He stepped slowly away from the two men, eyes riveted to the ground for something of interest.

Kevin half-watched him depart, then returned his full attention to Kawamura.

"What I can tell you, Mr. Whitehouse, is that your old man was proficient with explosives, because this job would have taken a lot of time and careful preparation. The way the evidence lays out right now, he wanted to destroy this garage of his and himself with it. He must have been hiding something here that he couldn't risk ever being found."

"Something like what?"

"I have no idea. Police Chief Carville is bringing bulldozers here tomorrow to excavate two feet of dirt from the area of the garage and part of the backyard."

"For what reason?"

"They're looking for signs of an underground passage, a trap door, or human remains—possibly a mass grave."

Kevin was taken aback. "Are you suggesting that my father might have been a serial killer?"

"We're not suggesting anything yet, Mr. Whitehouse. We're just following protocol and doing what we are told."

"I understand that. Then can you send me a copy of your report when it's finished?"

Kawamura thought for a moment before nodding his assent. "Give me your address, and I'll have my assistant messenger a copy to you. This isn't within your jurisdiction, but I'll extend you a professional courtesy because your father was involved. But the next time I'm in New York City and I look you up, remember, you owe me one."

"You got it." After they exchanged contact information, Kevin looked around for David, whom he saw off in the distance, staring down at his feet. Kevin quickly closed the gap between them, and when he caught up, he too looked at the ground to see what had captured his friend's attention. "What's the matter? Lose something? Find something?"

"Nah, I was just thinking," David said. "Let's just play devil's advocate and go the wrong way that this case is pointing in, meaning let's just say that your father *was* in some sort of trouble, maybe he knew something and was killed to shut him up." David stopped, frowning and shaking his head. "But that doesn't work either because why the shaped charges? Why give a fuck about the house?"

"Maybe they had my father wire the house while at gunpoint."

"Could be...could be...if this was life on *Mars!* Who in their right mind would do all this work at gunpoint?"

"What if the bombs were a defensive mechanism made to provide protection if his enemies ever got the drop on him?"

"*Protection?* You protect yourself by killing the other guy. Let me ask you: How many murders per year do you think a town like this averages?"

"I don't really know. Something like one every six months to a year," Kevin guessed. "It's not like New York—heavily populated, multiethnic, with everybody on top of each other. Here, I would guess, murder is infrequent."

Well, when I was at the Rutland morgue earlier, they had a fresh body, a man recently bludgeoned to death, time of death still to be determined. I'm wondering if the two murders—that is, *if* your father was murdered—are connected."

Having said his piece, David started back to the car with Kevin alongside him.

"Yeah, I heard about someone else getting killed. It came as a shock to Carville, too. But at best you could be grasping at straws, buddy."

"Grasping at straws? Haven't you ever heard the axiom that death comes in threes?"

"I honestly think you need a very big drink, my friend."

THE DEADBEAT CLUB

David awoke first, and was already out the door and on his way to town. Since Kevin had been sleeping soundly, he decided not to wake him. The morning was cool and the sun shone brightly above the high trees framing the parking area. David inhaled lungsful of the fresh clean air before he climbed into the car.

Up on Route 7 North, at the turn on Center Street, was a pharmacy mostly empty this early in the morning. He turned into the lot, and a few beats later he was through the double doors, making a beeline for the newspaper section. He grabbed the local paper and began rifling through it, searching for information on Richard Whitehouse's death. There was a brief mention a few pages in about the explosion at his home, and that the body found among the debris was undoubtedly his.

He also found an article about another murder, this one slightly more detailed than the one about Kevin's father. Trip Hepner, otherwise known as Glitter-Gun because of his near-legendary reputation as the town jeweler, had been found dead two nights ago. Since Hepner's office had been thoroughly ransacked, the insurance companies were combing through the wreckage to ascertain the value of the jewelry taken. Many precious gems were left behind, while the contents of a display case of cubic zirconium had been snatched. Obviously, Hepner's attacker had no knowledge of gemology, since he simply grabbed anything that just looked expensive. But the investigation so far suggested another explanation: that the robbery was bogus, merely a cover-up for the murder of Glitter-Gun.

David went over to the self-service coffee counter and poured two cups: black, no sugar. His next stop was the stationary aisle, where he found a roll of clear Scotch tape. He went up to the cash register with the newspaper conspicuously tucked under his arm, paid for everything and left. When he was back behind the wheel, he paused for a moment to put the cups in the cup holders, and then drove off. Soon he was back at the motel parking lot and killed the engine. He picked up one of the coffees and took small sips of the oily hot liquid as he reread the story about the murdered jeweler.

It was then that he spotted a patrol car turning into the lot that stopped in front of their motel room door. David held the paper up to his face, peering over the top to observe an older man emerge from his vehicle. The man paused for a moment to hitch up his heavy belt and holster harness, adjust his ten-gallon hat, and then step aside to shut the door. From the passenger side, a lean young man got out, wearing an identical hat and uniform, his posture a dead giveaway for his lack of confidence.

The two men approached the door to Kevin's motel room, rapping on it roughly. Kevin's face emerged, squinting as his eyes were assaulted by the bright sunlight. He put a hand up to his forehead to block the glare, nodded to several of the officers' questions, and then invited them in. David put the newspaper on the passenger's seat, took another sip of his coffee, and got out. After a quick look around, he strode over to the motel room door and pressed his ear against it to eavesdrop on the conversation.

"I have a bad feeling about this, Whitehouse," Chief Carville said, hooking his thumbs behind his belt as he paced back and forth in front of Kevin. "I've got a New York police detective... no... make that two, snooping around and poking their noses in everyone's business here. You want to dig and dig, invite the media, and bring a shit-storm of negative opinion down on this town."

"You can't be serious," Kevin said. "You sound like you think *we* put the bombs in my father's garage."

"No, but your father did."

"Look, Chief, you have *two* murders here in the space of seven days. What do you think—that whatever the hell is going on here will blow over and that will be the end of it?"

"Yeah, and why shouldn't it?"

Kevin went over to the window, parted the curtains, and stared out unseeing while he collected his thoughts. "I shouldn't have to point out that you're in the business of apprehending criminals, not protecting tourism in your sleepy old town. You don't yet know *why* these murders happened. You have no clue *why* either of these people are dead, and since that's the case, you don't know if these murders are going to stop or not."

"I don't need *you* to tell me that, *High-Powered*. I know

how to do my job. You think just because it was your father who was killed, you have some sort of familial jurisdiction here? Your father was a suicide, Kevin."

"He was no suicide."

Carville went silent for a moment, the expression on his face softening as he looked at Kevin before he resumed. "Alright, we have all of Rutland's C.S.I. digging up and around the bombsite. Their department resources are over-taxed helping us. We also have Glitter-Gun here, beaten to death. The clues to his murder are just starting to come in. So sure, we could use the help in working one or both of these cases. So I called your captain Jeffries in New York City to see what he thought about our deputizing you while you're up here."

"David, too?"

"Yes, you and your colleague." Carville reached into his back pocket and retrieved a case that contained a silver shield on one side and an ID card on the other. He handed it over to Kevin. "So… will you help?"

"Certainly," Kevin said as he shoved the ID into his back pocket. "But what about David's?"

Deputy Peppard handed him another case that held the same two items.

"That one's for Mr. Allerton," Carville said.

"I'll make sure he gets it."

"Do you know where you plan to start?"

"My gut instinct tells me we should check out the jewelry store first."

"Okay. Well, stay in touch and happy hunting."

His presence obscured by some nearby shrubbery, David watched the squad car exit the parking lot. He retrieved the newspaper and the untouched coffee from the car, and headed to the motel room. He found Kevin sitting on the bed, staring off into space.

"Carville ticked you off?" David asked as he went over to his friend and handed him the cup of coffee.

Holding the coffee in one hand, Kevin picked up the case from the bed with the other and gave it to David.

"It doesn't contain a photograph," David said after examining the case with a bemused smile. "Anyone could use this to impersonate a deputy."

Ignoring the comment and indicating the newspaper, Kevin asked, "So, anything in there about either death?"

"Just all the news that's fit to print."

"Such as, may I ask?" Kevin pried off the top and slowly sipped his coffee.

David sat down on the other bed and began tearing the paper carefully. "First, we have the article on your father's murder. Mostly fluff. They don't even mention the likelihood of finding hundreds of bodies when they do the excavation…like *that's* going to happen. But what coverage should we expect by now—really—he blew up almost a week ago."

"Yeah, so what else is new?"

David retrieved the roll of tape from his pants pocket and taped the article to the wall. "Voilà!"

"Then what?" Kevin asked.

"The jewelry owner, of course."

"What makes you think they're connected?" Kevin continued, sounding skeptical.

"Because this is a small-ass town. Two major crimes in a small-ass town got to be connected somewhere, somehow," David explained as he sat down on the edge of the bed again to painstakingly tear out the second article. "I've got a dude on the inside of Rutland's forensics department who can hopefully provide us with more information than the little we got from the fire department."

"I have the fire department report right here." Kevin picked it up from the nightstand between the beds and waved it at David. "It was just delivered today by messenger from Kawamura—the fire chief—while you were gone. Too bad there's no kitchen table to stack this stuff on like we do at home, only this little itty-bitty nightstand."

"We've got something better, my friend." David stood, removing a small decorative picture from the wall to make room for the article about Trip Hepner's death, which he taped up near the first.

"Is this supposed to be helping us, David?"

"Yeah—I saw it done in a movie once," he said as he walked over to Kevin to retrieve the fire chief's report so he could tape it, too, to the wall. Then he stepped back to admire his handiwork.

"So you're going to explore a connection?" Kevin asked.

"Yes, and I'll start by going back to the morgue again tonight."

"Why?"

"The blows to the jeweler's body looked funky. Something doesn't seem right. I'm wondering what the M.E. report will say."

Kevin was rummaging through his shoulder bag for his reading glasses. After he found them and put them on, he got up to read the article about his father. "I think there's something significant still there, in the wreckage."

"Kevin, you can forget about that. The bulldozers are churning over all of that rubble even as we speak."

"Well, then they might actually uncover something very important."

"Like what? Human skulls?"

Kevin frowned at David, but before he could say anything else there was a knock on the door.

Both men froze.

The knock came a second time.

"Uhhh... who's gonna answer it?" David said.

"You're the one closest to the door," Kevin pointed out.

David went over to his bed to grab a carryall from beside it that contained a Browning Mark III. He snapped out the magazine to see if it was loaded, slapped it back in, and then pulled back on the action to make sure there was a bullet in the chamber. He walked to the door, and then positioned his back against the threshold. "Who is it?"

The answer was just a series of insistent knocks.

Finally, David moved to unlock the door and swung it open to reveal a woman who marched through the opening, right past David, heading for the middle of the room. After she'd stormed in, David slammed the door shut behind her.

"DAVID!" Margaret shouted into the air after whipping around to look at him, startled by the report of the door, the sight of him, *and* the gun.

"Well, well, well. How on earth did you find us?" he asked calmly.

"Kevin called me yesterday and gave me directions," she

growled, pushing a lock of lustrous brown hair away from her eyes. "I should have known that you'd be up here, too. What's wrong? New York's too lonely for you with your playmate gone?"

"Sounds like the lyrics to *your* song, Em."

"I've asked you not to call me that."

"Right." David nodded with a chuckle.

Margaret tossed her long, dark mane defiantly and approached Kevin, allowing his arms to envelope her in a welcoming embrace.

"This is such a charming little New England town, don't you think?" she asked him.

"Yes, it is. I just haven't had a chance to notice much. I've been busy with the case," he said, kissing her lightly on the forehead as he let her go.

"I can see that," Margaret said, as her eyes wandered over to the wall where the makeshift map of the case was shaping up. "When is your father's funeral?"

"Very soon."

"So, that pokes a hole in your romantic weekend, huh, Em?" David asked derisively.

Margaret glanced at David briefly before she addressed Kevin. "Do you want me to go with you?"

"Only in spirit. The funeral will be a time for my family to mourn his passing. That's if they do mourn him. I don't want to detract from it by bringing my entourage from New York."

"Well, then let's hit a few area restaurants. How about we go to breakfast right now?"

"Yeah, but remember, Margaret, I'm on a case here and not a vacation."

"I get it, I get it. Now let's find an IHOP or something."

While Margaret and Kevin went out for breakfast, David was ready for some hard-core police work. He headed over to the local telephone company office—via car service taxi—and asked to see the records of the calls made by both Richard Whitehouse Jr. and Trip Hepner on the day of their deaths. A kindly, mature woman by the name of Theresa took him on an informal tour of the facilities before fulfilling his specific request. It seemed obvious to David that she wasn't used to having visitors during her shift, and was thrilled to have someone—especially from the police—acknowledge her importance by soliciting her help.

Finally, David gently nudged her to cut to the chase, so she sat down at her terminal and accessed the database to create a report based on David's search parameters. The computer network was slow and the printers were anything but cutting edge; still, they accomplished their jobs just the same. After handing over the printouts to him, she let him use the conference room so he'd be comfortable while he reviewed the information. This was good. By remaining on the premises, he could get clarification as needed, as well as obtain further data if what he had proved insufficient. All in all, David realized, this promised to be a long morning.

First IHOP, now this?" Margaret asked, indicating the construction trucks parked along the road as they approached his father's house. Her remark was intended to convey her disappointment at the way her first few hours in pictur-esque New England were being spent—or squandered, as she framed it in her mind.

"I want to be on top of what they've got so far," Kevin explained, as they waited for a bulldozer blocking the drive-way to finish up so they could gain access to it.

"Why don't you just wait for the reports like you used to?" Margaret suggested. She looked around in dismay, bit-ing her lower lip.

"This is faster. Plus, I'll still get any reports outstand-ing—as well as updates on the ones I have—as they become available."

Still gazing at her, Kevin was, as usual, smitten with her beauty: her graceful patrician features, deep blue eyes, and luxuriant brunette tresses. While he knew she was born into one of Manhattan's so-called high society families, she sel-dom offered any details. In fact, he was only aware of her elitist connections because she was such a shameless name-dropper. She would, from time to time, tell him of meeting some important person, but could never impress him be-cause he would not know most of them. He was amused—albeit wickedly—by her reaction to being present at the ex-cavation site. He knew she'd be very reluctant to venture outside the car with so much dirt and debris loose in the air.

When the way was clear, Kevin turned the car into the driveway and parked in a large, beaten-earth lot just in front of the rise. "I want to talk to the foreman in charge of the dig-ging operation. It shouldn't take long."

"Sure, go ahead," Margaret replied eagerly, relieved that he didn't ask her to accompany him.

Kevin slipped out of the car and walked across the gritty

dirt, until he'd mounted the crest of the rise to witness the scene below, which was swarming with men and machines. Excavators were piling up heaps of dirt in the backyard, while backhoes extracted enormous loads of earth from the center of the blast crater.

Kevin made his way down to the fringes of the operation. There he encountered a clique of men wearing white hard hats, save for one who wore a ten-gallon hat. There was no mistaking Chief Carville, who was engaged in a jovial conversation until he noticed Kevin's approach. The smile vanished from his face, as he abruptly recomposed his features and turned to the business at hand.

"Well, Mr. Whitehouse..." Carville said, while managing to eke out a new smile for Kevin, "it's good to see you this morning."

"Good to see you too, Chief. Anything significant turn up?" Kevin asked, squinting against the sun's rays that seemed directly aimed at his eyes.

"We just got started. Haven't found a thing yet," Carville said as he looked around, then back to the men surrounding him. "Sorry, where are my manners!" he exclaimed. "Everyone, I would like you to meet Richard's son, Kevin Whitehouse. He's a big-time detective from NYC."

"Oh, is that a fact?" one of the hard hats replied in a somewhat mocking tone. He was a sturdy robust fellow with an angular face and a long nose, and his eyes twinkled with amusement. He sported a beard and mustache, comingled with gray.

"This is Leo Desantis," Carville explained, "the town comptroller."

"Pleased to meet you," Kevin said as they shook hands.

"Your father was a really good guy, Kevin—and great at his job. He blasted away miles of rock for several of our building projects. It's a shame he had to go out like this," Desantis said.

"A shame," Kevin repeated.

Carville pointed to another man, tall and lanky, dressed in a suit and tie, who wore stylish black-rimmed glasses. He had a thick mane of gray hair, the finishing touch on his distinctively urbane appearance. "And this is Harold Klein. He handles the legal work for Brandon—town business."

Klein reached out and shook his hand, too.

"If you ever need a lawyer, I'm one of the few around here. So you can find me easily enough in the local yellow pages."

"Thanks, I'll remember that."

"Finally, meet Darryl Bates, ace reporter, Channel Eight news." Carville nodded in the direction of a somber-looking man, younger than the others, with very symmetrical features, including an uncommonly straight nose and piercing brown eyes. But when he looked over at Kevin and smiled, his entire face lit up.

Kevin leaned across the distance between them to shake his hand. "What are *you* hoping to find, Mr. Bates?"

"Well, with an apology in advance to you and your father—may he rest in peace—I hope to find a graveyard filled with victims," he said unabashedly.

"Kind of a ghoulish expectation, wouldn't you say, Darryl?" Leo Desantis said.

"Ghoulishness sells newspapers and gets you airtime," Bates quipped.

Addressing Carville, Kevin reiterated, "So like you said before, there's nothing yet." After hearing Bates' speculation, Kevin felt like he needed some reassurance; he wanted to make sure he'd heard Carville right the first time.

"Sorry, but that's correct," Carville replied. "This operation looks like a dead end. In fact, I'm going to wrap it up in a few hours. It's too expensive to keep going with nothing to show for it."

"It looks as though your father's death was simply an unfortunate accident," Desantis said. "He was doing what he liked to do best, so at least he died happy."

"That's an ironic remark, 'died happy,' " Kevin said with a smirk.

"How about you, *High-Powered*—any leads yet?" Carville asked Kevin in a challenging tone.

"Nothing yet. We're still studying the data we have," Kevin replied evenly.

"You mean you can't bring up your science boys from New York, with their laser devices and mobile labs to piece all this shit together in twenty minutes like they do on television?"

Kevin chuckled. "Trust me—they would never pull out all the stops for someone like my father. He was just your average Joe Blow."

"Your father was no average Joe," Leo Desantis said flatly. "Every year on the Fourth of July he would put on the most incredible fireworks show you could possibly imagine. He loved doing it for the kids. It was his pride and joy to come up with a whole new array of lights and sounds. And he did it all for nothing. Not one thin dime."

"Now, could you say that about yourself, Harold?" Bates jabbed an elbow playfully into Klein's ribs.

"What are you talking about? I take pro bono cases," Klein replied, sounding insulted.

"Well, gentlemen, I've got some work to do here," Carville said as he doffed his ten-gallon hat and strode off toward a backhoe that was standing motionless.

Kevin looked around the site and then at the house, where he noticed Margaret climbing the steps to the porch. Kevin was shocked that she'd left the car, but evidently she'd found her way quickly to an area that was relatively unscathed.

"Excuse me, gentlemen," Kevin said as he left the group, heading back to the driveway to pick up the gravel path that bordered the side of the house. When he got there, he found the porch deserted and the front door slightly ajar. He slowly pushed the door open, and stepped inside the house where he grew up. First, he entered the den, lined with bookshelves and furnished with a comfortable sofa and plump armchairs. Standing lamps were strategically placed around the room for the sole purpose of providing ample light for reading. He noticed two were askew, probably from the shock of the explosion.

Kevin's memories floated through the room, images of his father and mother together in the den; then his mother on the couch reading, his father standing at the window staring out at the yard. How could so much stillness, so much nothing, hold him for so long? His mother and his father never seemed close or passionate. They were a cold couple. He remembered his mother showering him and his brother with love, but could not recall a single instance where he witnessed his parents demonstrating any affection for each other.

He moved further into the house, into the corridor that branched off from the kitchen, led to the bathroom, and ended with the bedrooms. Kevin opened one of the bedroom doors, and was surprised to find Margaret standing there, her back to him.

"What are you doing?" he asked.

She turned around to face him with a framed photograph in her hand. "Is this your family?"

As Kevin stepped closer, his eyes locked on the small picture in the silver frame. It instantly conjured up memories of fishing trips in the nearby pine forests along Lake Hortonia. He reached for the photo and gazed at it fondly. He remembered experiencing the great outdoors with his father and brother, when they would all fish together until the sun settled. His father liked it because it kept his sons quiet and occupied. Once he helped them to set their lines, he could just sit and drink a beer or two and not have to utter a word. Kevin and Simon focused on the task at hand, vying with each other as little—and as quietly—as possible; because if they got too boisterous, a glare from their father could feel worse than a lash.

"Yeah, these are my parents: my mother, Claire, my father, Richard, me and my older brother, Simon."

"I've never heard you mention Simon before. What happened to him?" Margaret asked.

"He joined the military to get away from my dad. We never heard from him after that."

"Do you think he'll be coming to the funeral?"

"I don't know—and anyway, I'm done here." Kevin rested the photograph on the dresser.

"You don't want to keep it?" Margaret asked.

"No," Kevin said before he turned around to leave the room.

Thinking he might feel differently at a later date, Margaret slipped the framed photo into her jacket pocket for safekeeping, and then followed him out.

"Where to now?" she asked his back.

"The crime scene at the jewelry store, where this guy Hepner was just murdered. If David's right and it's connected to my father's death, there might be a clue there, something that's been overlooked."

"Well then, let's go before it gets too late."

They made their way past a large earth mover that was rumbling alongside them, to where their car was parked in the dirt lot.

Theresa opened the door to the conference room and peered in at David as he was reviewing the phone records.

"Sir, is there anything I can get for you? Coffee? Tea? A sandwich, perhaps?"

"Do you have a yellow marker and a reverse telephone directory I could use?" David asked.

"Certainly, I'll be right back," she said as she stepped back and closed the door gently.

David believed that a case could always be made less difficult by checking the most obvious details first, such as those that phone records could provide. While on the face of it they were just numbers, they sometimes possessed a magical ability to tie individuals together who were in all other respects total strangers. David had the estimated time of the explosion on the Whitehouse property, so he checked all the incoming and outgoing calls to and from Richard's phone leading up to that time. Armed with this information, he could make a list of suspects in minutes.

But the problem was that Kevin's father made so few phone calls: one was to an automated recording of the local weather, another was to what appeared to be an out-of-state relative, and another was to the local market, undoubtedly to have his groceries delivered. There were no suspects to be found here; these were just simple calls that led nowhere. Then a creeping doubt began to form in David's mind. Maybe Richard Whitehouse was only too aware of the police tactic of scouring phone records, so long ago he could have decided to use a burner phone for the sake of anonymity, es-chewing his home phone. Otherwise, considering the scant number of calls in the days before his death, he appeared to be severely withdrawn and solitary, qualities that fit the profile of a suicide.

Glitter-Gun, however, was another matter altogether. Trip Hepner made a dozen calls on his mobile phone the day he was killed, before they stopped abruptly after the time of his death. He'd also received several calls—with only one lasting longer than a minute. It was David's guess that these were all business as usual.

After Theresa brought him the reverse lookup directory, he flipped through the phone numbers in numerical order to find the names and addresses of their owners, and made a note of each one on the printouts. When he was finished, he stashed the pages in his pocket as he rose to leave the conference room. On his way out, he thanked Theresa for all her help, and managed to leave before she could embroil him in any further conversation.

Once outside, David resumed pondering the circumstances around Richard Whitehouse's death. For example, the lack of a suicide note—not that much of anything could have survived the fiery explosion that rocked his garage. But there was also the lack of any contact whatsoever with anyone who might help provide an explanation or justification for his actions. David was forced to conclude that the man was in such a deep depression he excluded everyone from his life, that all he wanted to do was expire.

But how might his death coincide with the death of Trip Hepner? Did a situation involving Richard Whitehouse cause a chain reaction that cost Hepner his life, too? So with that in mind, David decided the next target of his investigation should be the jewelry store.

Since Kevin was chauffeuring Margaret around—and since the rental car was in his name—David arranged for a taxi to take him into town. As he sat in the backseat, he contemplated the buildings that stretched along the commercial thoroughfare: new storefronts of brick and white wood with large floor-to-ceiling display windows, their sidewalks bordered by small trees and well-tended shrubbery. Before he knew it, the cab had stopped at his destination.

Two police officers flanked the entrance to the jewelry store, and stepped forward to meet David when they noticed him approaching. He reached into his jacket immediately and produced his official Brandon PD Identification. After a quick glance, the officers nodded and allowed him entry. Everything in the circular front showroom looked normal, save for the fact that the display cases were empty. He took out his IC recorder and started to describe the eerily undisturbed aspect of the space, which was clearly not the scene of the altercation. The jewelry must have been removed before the assailant entered and met with the victim in another room in the shop. David walked on, through the doorway ahead, to where the C.S.I. team was working. He was surprised to see Kevin and Margaret there, too—Kevin standing over the technicians, while Margaret stood quietly at his side.

The office showed all the evidence of having been the scene of a violent struggle: ledgers, catalogs, broken lamps, and other objects were strewn all over the floor, tables and chairs were overturned, and surprisingly large splatters of blood were everywhere.

When Kevin spotted David, he went over to him and said in low tones, "It looks like either Glitter-Gun had a vicious enemy—or he had something he wasn't going to part with easily."

"Why? Because this looks like it started as a beating and grew into a murderous bludgeoning?" David whispered, looking around.

"Yeah, you start small, then work your way up to the climax. Which also explains the disarray. Apparently, when the interrogation didn't work, the assailant ransacked the room for the answers Hepner wasn't giving him."

"Do you think he found what he was looking for?" David asked.

Before Kevin could answer, Margaret appeared at Kevin's side, looking down as she nervously straightened her dress.

"After this, I can never accuse you of not taking me out on a memorable date—that's for sure."

Kevin shrugged his shoulders. "I'm sorry, Margaret; as I explained before, the murder that happened here might be tied in somehow with my dad's death." His tone was apologetic.

"He's a detective first and a lover boy later, Em, especially since this case involves his father," David said with equanimity. "The attention you're seeking from him will have to come after the corpses, explosions, bloodstains—etcetera."

"I don't believe that, or I wouldn't be with him," Margaret replied defensively, her one-track mind on overdrive.

"Margaret, you are *so* codependent, you should have the word tattooed on your forehead," David said angrily.

"Alright you two," Kevin broke in. "Please, let's just get along. Can we do that?"

"You know, I never start with her," David said, placing a hand over his heart, in a gesture of innocence. "It's just that sometimes she comes out with the most thoughtless remarks, as if we *enjoy* standing around blood-splattered crime scenes…"

"Are you the detective assigned to this case?" a C.S.I. investigator asked David from across the room. He was standing in the corner where the body was found amid a copious amount of blood.

"Yes, I am," David replied. "David Allerton."

"I've found something that I think you ought to see."

David gave Margaret a courteous nod, and turned away from the couple to join the two C.S.I. technicians who were sifting through bloodied shards of broken glass and splintered wood. The one who'd summoned him held up a sizable evidence bag.

"What's up?" David asked.

"My name is Cappers, sir. We found this yesterday."

"What exactly is it?"

Cappers handed it over to David so he could see it close up: it was the square, heavy metal base of a lamp, carefully wrapped in a clear evidence bag. "We think the base of this lamp was used to crush Mr. Hepner's skull." He took it back and held the base up over his head for a moment to show the downward swing. "He could have used it like a rock and railed away on Mr. Hepner's head while holding it like this."

"Really?" David remarked as he stared up at the object in the bag.

"And we've gotten latents off of it. Not just partials, but full latents." Cappers sounded excited as he conveyed this information.

"Cappers, I would suggest that you drop everything else, and get your guys to work on identifying these finger-prints," David said.

"We expect to have those answers later today," Cappers assured him. He handed the lamp base over to David who took it away almost reluctantly.

David nodded thoughtfully. "Oh, okay… in fact, that's great."

The conversation over, Cappers moved to another part of the room to continue searching for further evidence.

David could feel the murderous weight of the lamp base in his hand as he looked around for Kevin and Margaret.

But apparently they'd left. He wondered if it was his presence that caused them to leave precipitously. He didn't have anything against Margaret, per se—it was just that she threw off Kevin's priorities. Finally, with the fingerprints, they had what looked like a hot lead—the hottest lead so far. And where was his partner? Out chasing Margaret's shapely ass.

After giving Cappers his contact information, David placed the evidence bag with the lamp base on top of the desk and left the technicians to finish up their work. He passed through the showroom and stopped in the doorway to ask a question of the officers still standing guard. "Did you see a well-dressed man and woman leave here just a few minutes ago?"

They thought about it for a second, looked at each other and then shook their heads. "No. But they might have gotten past us," one replied.

"People get by you?" David asked incredulously.

"Sir, we're not too concerned about who leaves the premises and with what. We are more interested in who enters and with what. We are interdiction, not incarceration."

David nodded and said, "I understand." Then he continued on to the street, until he noticed a cab dropping off a fare a few yards away. He dashed over to the driver's-side window and asked, "Can I get a lift with you?"

The driver sighed. "Where to?"

Willie hamilton had his head under the hood of his vintage Ford pickup truck, trying to get the carburetor linkage to pull back far enough to open the throttle all the way. When he stepped back from the open hood of the vehicle, he was

bathed in the overhead floodlights that also lit up his battered red-roofed, white-walled trailer home. He wiped his
hands thoroughly on his hand towel until it turned black,
then went around to the back of the truck, lowered the gate
and reached into the twelve-pack for another cold beer. He
found the carton empty.

He ambled over to his trailer home and went up the short
flight of stairs to the front door, now covered over with a
wooden board that substituted for the glass that had been
broken. As he entered his living room, he was surprised to
find "Cigarette Burns" sitting in the one easy chair, his back
to him, watching TV and drinking a beer.

"Cigarette—what the fuck are you doing here?" Willie
asked.

Cigarette turned around to regard him over the chair
back. "I just came over to talk."

His face was recently shaved, his eyes sharp and dark,
his shoulders squared tightly as if he'd spent years in the
military. His straight hair was short and buzzed flat on top.

"About what?" Unperturbed, Willie walked over to the
refrigerator behind the counter that separated the kitchen
from the living room. Inside the icebox he found a cold bottle
of beer. As he held it, he noticed his hand starting to tremble.
"About what, Cigarette?" he repeated. "Are you making a
run for it, too?"

"You could say that." Cigarette rose from the easy chair
to his full height, being quite tall, and watched Willie closely as he said, "Glitter-Gun was found dead the other day,
buddy."

"Yeah, I heard."

"Did you have anything to do with that?"

Willie twisted the cap off the beer bottle. "I had nothing to do with it."

"How about this, then? Are you banging Katherine Werthers?"

"You know that's none of your business."

"You beat the shit out of Glitter-Gun just to get where he hid the diamonds, so that you and Kat can run off with them."

"That's not true, Cigarette. All we were looking for was our share," Willie explained dejectedly, upset at being so misunderstood.

Cigarette sauntered over to the counter, leaning over it to get right in Willie's face, placing his beer bottle down on the countertop. "But the deal was to wait *five* years for the heat to fade from the heist—*not three!*" his voice rising.

"But we need the money *now*, Cigarette," Willie said as he took a long draw from his beer, mentally calculating his chances of overpowering Cigarette in any physical contest that might ensue. While they were roughly the same height and weight, Cigarette's mass came from fat and Willie's from muscle. Also, his would-be opponent had been a heavy smoker for years—hence, his nickname. Willie had age on his side as well—he was almost twenty-five years younger than Cigarette. But still he wondered if the old man could beat him.

Cigarette Burns was a good second man on a heist, and could keep his cool in the face of the most precarious conditions. He was cool now, like ice water, especially judging from the look in his eyes as he stared across the counter. However, Willie was also aware that Cigarette would not take kindly to his killing of Glitter-Gun for whatever reason. Underneath that calm exterior lay an undoubtedly super-heated interior, boiling over at the thought that Willie had something to do with Glitter-Gun's death. Although Cigarette kept mostly to himself, Glitter was a close friend— they had been good buddies since childhood. On the other hand, Willie was just the town misfit, and might have meant little or nothing to Cigarette.

"So," Cigarette began, "let me get this right. You claim you didn't beat Glitter-Gun that night. Then, let me ask you, who do you think did? Maybe Katherine has a man you don't know about who's helping her nab the stash for them?"

"No, she would never do that," Willie said, taking another pull from the bottle.

"Listen, Willie—you claim you didn't kill Glitter-Gun, and yet you talk about needing the money from the Franklin heist. Now here's the question: how the hell are you going to find the diamonds now? Glitter-Gun was the only one who knew where they were." Cigarette Burns rapped the countertop with a fingertip for emphasis.

"I have a ballpark idea as to where the diamonds are stashed."

"And how did you get that? In your sleep?"

"Let's just say that I had an epif... an epiph—"

Cutting him off, Cigarette said, "So you had a vision from on high, huh? Or did you happen to get this epiphany while you were beating Glitter-Gun to death?"

Willie leaned back, away from the counter and against the refrigerator. He played with the bottle in his hands. "I didn't have a... whatever. I went over to Glitter-Gun's shop and roughed him up a bit, but I didn't beat him to death, Cigarette."

"He's dead, Willie, and he certainly didn't die from a little horseplay. So why don't you grow a pair of balls and tell me what really happened?"

Turning the bottle up, Willie swallowed the rest of his beer in one last gulp. He was debating what he would say next. If he told the truth, how would Cigarette Burns take the news? If he took it the wrong way, would Willie be able to handle him? Although he was a quiet man and mostly a loner, quiet motherfuckers can be quite dangerous.

Willie searched the trailer in his mind for something suitable to defend himself with—if it came to that. Finally, he said, "Look, the man had more stones in him than I thought. He wouldn't talk. All he kept doing was passing out. I finally crowned him with a lamp part and he went all dreamy."

"He went dreamy..." Cigarette repeated in a mocking tone.

"Yeah, as if he'd taken a hit of some sorta drug," Willie added.

"You popped him in the head with a lamp, retard! Glitter-Gun and I go way back. You didn't figure me in your equation, did you?" Cigarette Burns continued to lean across the counter, almost as if he was preparing to launch himself over it.

Willie began to strangle the neck of the beer bottle in his hands. "I know you're old friends," Willie said. "I was close to him, too."

"Yeah, you were as close to him as a horse's snout is to its ass."

"What's that supposed to mean?"

"You killed him. You killed a good friend of mine, maybe my best friend."

"You have no friends, Cigarette," Willie smiled. "You are a lone wolf. You got into this on your own, by yourself, without a family or a friend. Don't come to my home and whine about Glitter-Gun. You didn't care about him, never did. He was holding our loot—that's the long and short of it."

"And you killed him because of that?"

"I didn't mean to kill him; I just wanted to hurt him enough so he'd tell me where the diamonds were. Instead, he got out his gun, and after that all hell broke loose because I needed a weapon, too. Finally, I slugged him really hard, partly in self-defense because I was afraid he might shoot me. After that, he went all dreamy and fell to the floor. That's the God's honest truth."

"Oh, so now you think I'm a dumb fuck and I'll let all that pass?"

"C'mon, Cigarette, I think you're overreacting."

Cigarette Burns finally stopped leaning over the counter. He stood up and pointed outside. "You're working on your shitty truck out there at all hours of the night, so you and Kat can use it to go grab the loot and leave town like a pair of lovebirds. But you forget there are others involved in this mess, and some of us want our cut just as much as you do."

"I'm going to give *everyone* their cut, Cigarette, after we take out ours." After lurching away from the refrigerator, Willie walked steadily along the length of the counter and toward the front door.

"Oh, so Glitter-Gun *did* tell you where you could find the diamonds before he died," Cigarette said as he followed Willie to the door, closing the gap between them.

"Yeah, he did—well, er… just approximately where they are. We're going digging tonight and you're invited. That's if you want to come." Willie paused to face Cigarette, to gauge his reaction.

"Getting an invite for my share is like asking permission to wipe my own ass, Willie." Cigarette pulled a pack of smokes from his pocket, knocked one out and slipped it between his lips. "Where are the shov—?"

The bottom edge of Willie's beer bottle, which he'd never let go of, cut through the air and made contact with Cigarette's forehead, catching him on the temple with such force that the glass shattered. Cigarette went down on his hands and knees, his forehead cut and bleeding profusely, the blow leaving him momentarily stunned. Willie took advantage of that opportunity to drive a sweeping kick from his steel-toed boot into Cigarette's ribs, causing him to cough explosively and roll over onto his back.

Then Willie was off, tearing through his front door and around back to the gas meters. Grabbing a nearby pipe wrench, he loosened one of the feeder hoses, allowing the gas to escape. He pulled up and pushed the hose end into the house through the half-opened kitchen window and closed the window, hoping to trap the gas inside. Then he dashed into his shed that resembled a tin outhouse, and grabbed two shovels. When he emerged, he looked around briefly—checking for signs of Cigarette's presence—and then hurled the shovels into the back of the truck and closed the gate.

Still in a mad panic, Willie hurried to the front of the vehicle and slammed down the hood before he leaped behind the wheel. To his vast relief, the engine caught almost immediately, and he steered the truck out of the space and onto the dirt road that bordered the trailer. As he drove off, he caught a glimpse of Cigarette Burns staggering out of the doorway of his home, holding his forehead to staunch the bleeding. Willie laughed to himself as he rumbled past, making a sharp left turn that would take him to the main road.

At almost the same moment, Cigarette Burns braced himself against the threshold of the doorframe for support and lobbed a dark object at the rear of the truck that just made it into the flatbed's enclosure. It rolled around and knocked against the shovels, but the noise it made wasn't loud enough for Willie to hear. A few seconds later, heralded by a sudden flash and an earsplitting boom, the fragmentation grenade that had become lodged in the corner of the flatbed behind the front seat detonated. The explosion ripped through the back of the cab, propelling steel fragments into Willie's back and belly. There was some fire and a lot of smoke, while cottony cushion bits filled the air like snow. Willie's eyes gaped open as a wave of coolness enveloped his midsection. He slumped over the steering wheel, losing control of the vehicle, which careened into a nearby tree with a loud bang.

The side of his head still running red, Cigarette staggered unsteadily across the dirt road and over to the smoking wreckage of the truck. In the meantime, Willie threw the weight of his shoulder against the driver's-side door to force it open and allow his body to fall out onto the soft shoulder of the roadway. Cigarette Burns headed directly for Willie and kneeled down to examine the extent of his wounds: the lower back of his T-shirt was a bloody, tangled mess with torn holes and jagged flesh. This wound was enough to signal the fact that his walking days were over.

"Listen, Willie, you need immediate medical attention," Cigarette said matter-of-factly. He reached down and grabbed him by the hands to roll him over onto his back and drag him back toward the house. Based on what he saw of his injuries, he knew Willie wouldn't feel much pain from such rough handling.

"Yeah, Cigarette, you've got to get me to a hospital," Willie pleaded weakly.

"First things first. Where did Glitter-Gun tell you the diamonds are stashed?"

"He didn't tell me... exactly."

"Then, why the shovels?" Cigarette persisted.

Willie moaned pitifully and then managed to say, "I was taking them out, just in case . . ."

"You just said before that he told you 'approximately' where to look. Now don't waste my time."

Instead of answering, Willie changed the subject. "Where are you taking me?"

"I'm taking you back to your house."

When they reached the bedraggled structure, Cigarette pulled Willie's body up the short flight of steps to his front door and into the living room.

Once inside, Willie smelled the gas. Panicking now, he screamed, "What the fuck, Cigarette? What do you want from me?!"

"I won't take you to a hospital until you tell me where you planned to dig," Cigarette threatened, kneeling over his head.

Willie struggled frantically to move, but to his horror he found that his legs would not obey him. "Okay, okay!" he shouted, remembering the gas. From where he lay on the floor, he could smell the odor of sulfur, making him crazy with fright. "He said the diamonds were at his home . . . near Lake Dunmore… ten miles north of here."

"He said they were *buried* somewhere—like buried treasure?" Cigarette asked.

"No, I told you already. I was taking the shovels just in case. All he said was that the diamonds were there."

"I bet," Cigarette remarked dubiously, as he stood up and crossed the small dining area to snatch the hand towel off the handle of the refrigerator. He wiped his bloody head and face with it, then tossed it on the counter before heading for the front door.

"What are you doing? Aren't you taking me to the hospital?" Willie called after him.

Cigarette stopped to turn around on his way down the stairs. "You've lost too much blood, kiddo. You'll never make it to a hospital."

"So! You're going to leave me here to suffocate on the gas and bleed to death?" Willie shouted. "Cigarette Burns, you schmuck!"

"Nah—I wouldn't do that to you," Cigarette mumbled under his breath as he put some distance between himself and the front of Willie's house. He retrieved a, palm-sized, green M67 hand grenade from his back pants pocket, holding the spoon on its side down firmly. With his other hand he snatched away the safety and then pulled the pin. He sent the spherical weapon airborne, the spoon flipping away as soon as it left his hand. The grenade followed a high trajectory before landing in the doorway and exploding, igniting the gas inside.

An angry fireball swelled at the threshold, crashing against the inside walls of the trailer and blowing out the windows, showering broken glass in all directions. The concussion from the blast almost knocked Cigarette off his feet, but he managed to dodge the burning debris as it spewed in all directions. At this point he realized he was far too close to the conflagration he'd unleashed, and made his way to his car in a low crouch, keeping his head down. A few beats later, the roof blew off in a deafening roar, sending burning shingles and fragments of rafters heavenward.

Cigarette Burns jumped into his Jeep and shifted into drive, peeling out and down the road, knowing full well that concerned citizens and the fire department would be up this way in a heartbeat. To avoid suspicion, he had to get off this single-lane dirt road and to the highway as soon as possible—and to his next destination, Lake Dunmore—as fast as his Jeep could fly.

A SUDDEN AVALANCHE OF CLUES

Margaret peered out the window of the diner at the small parking lot, the tarmac road beyond, and the wall of trees that bordered it. It was early in the morning with the sun still rising in a cloudless blue sky. She'd decided that she wanted a local country-style breakfast that would include some combination of bacon, sausages, eggs, potatoes, toast, waffles, and pancakes. Kevin, on the other hand, only wanted a cup of black coffee.

"Is that all you're going to have?" she asked him.

"I'm tired, not hungry," he explained.

"You will be, come twelve," Margaret retorted.

"Then I'll have a big lunch."

Margaret regarded the mountain of food on her plate with a broad smile. She'd ordered everything on the menu when she couldn't decide what to choose.

"Don't you think you have too many carbohydrates there? What with the hash browns *and* the pancakes?" Kevin asked innocently.

"No, I don't—and watch me eat it all," she chuckled, as she forked some scrambled eggs into her mouth. "Are you and David getting any closer to cracking this case for the poor police chief?"

"Poor police chief?" he repeated. "You should see *us*. We're not exactly pulling our own weight, either—we're out of our element here. For one thing, we don't have any PIs to shake down..."

"PIs?"

"Paid Informants. You ought to know that shorthand by now."

"They sound like they're crucial." Margaret cut a wedge out of her pancakes.

"They can be, especially when a case is stalled."

"So, are you saying that you're stalled?" Margaret asked, between bites. "David thinks there's a link between the murder of the jeweler and your father's death, doesn't he?"

"Yeah." Kevin reached over, took a piece of bacon from her plate and bit off the end.

"And is that simply because it happened here in the same town? What if it happened next month or a month ago— would it still feel connected?"

"It might. But it didn't. It happened days apart." Kevin pointed at her for emphasis with what was left of his bacon strip.

When there was a lull in the conversation, Margaret began attacking her plate with renewed vigor. "You need to think outside the box, then. Two men were murdered in cold blood—this is what you are thinking. This notion supports your belief that your father's death wasn't a suicide. He was killed for the same reason the jeweler was... because of some dark secret."

"That's right." Kevin nodded appreciatively at the precision of her assessment.

"Then what do these two have in common?"

Kevin didn't answer right away. He turned his head toward the window, gazing out at nothing while he mulled it over. "I don't know. I don't know these men—not even my own father. I have no clue about what he might have been up to, other than tinkering with explosive devices in his garage and putting on the Fourth of July fireworks show here in town."

"That's a shame," Margaret said softly. She put her fork down to reach across the table to stroke Kevin's cheek tenderly. "You loved your father in your own way, didn't you?"

"In my own way..." he repeated thoughtfully. "I guess you can say that."

She took away her hand. "Are you still going to go to his funeral?"

"That's the general plan."

"Do you want me to go?"

He looked at her. "Why do you keep asking?"

"I think you can use the moral support."

"No, thank you. You'll only cause a stir among my relatives, who will want to question the shit out of you about me and about our relationship and our New York lifestyle. I'd like you to meet them another time, when it's more appropriate—not at my father's funeral, don't you see?"

"You want to keep me hidden."

"No, that's not it at all. I want to keep you and David to myself. We have a job to do here and that's to find my father's killer. I'm here more for that than to bury him."

Kevin's cell phone started to ring from inside his jacket, startling the two of them. He looked at Margaret for tacit approval to answer, and she gave it to him wordlessly by returning to her breakfast.

Kevin popped the last piece of bacon between his fingers into his mouth, retrieved his cell, snapped it open and checked the screen. The caller was his uncle. "Yes, Uncle Nick," Kevin said.

"Kevin, it's your Uncle Nick."

"Yes, Uncle Nick," he repeated. The second time around, Kevin was exasperated. Didn't he hear him?

"Are you ready for the funeral tomorrow?"

"What do you mean?"

"Do you think you'll need anything? A tie? A good suit?"

"I'll be ready, Uncle Nick. What's the time?"

"Tomorrow morning at seven. Do you need a ride? I can have Paul there to pick you up at six thirty."

"That sounds like a plan. I'll be ready. Do you know why it's so early?"

"Funerals are usually pretty long. It starts at seven, but it probably won't be over until nine—and people hate to waste an entire day." His uncle paused, and then added, "It will be really good to see you there tomorrow. Your father would have been glad of your presence."

"I'm certain that he would."

An uncomfortable pause, then: "How are you feeling, Kevin. Are you okay?"

"I'm alright. I've gotta go now, Uncle Nick. I'm here with Margaret..."

"Oh! Is that your lady friend?"

"Yes."

"Please tell her I said hello, and that I'm sorry I didn't get a chance to meet her at the dinner. Is she going—?"

"I've really got to go, uncle. I'll talk to you later."

"Okay then, Kevin. You take care—"

"Talk soon." Kevin closed his cell and rested it on the table.

"Uncle Nick?" Margaret asked.

"Yeah, how could you tell?"

"You sounded like he was getting under your skin."

"A little."

"Why? Was he going on about your father?"

Kevin, looking distracted, shook his head. "What in the world did my father have in common with a jeweler?" he said, ignoring her question.

Margaret noticed, but let it go. "That's what you should be questioning now—figuring out what possible connection they could have with each other. Didn't David say something about fingerprints being lifted from the murder weapon?"

"Yeah."

"Well, you might have your answer sooner than you think once they can match those prints to the murderer," Margaret said hopefully. When she looked at Kevin to gauge his reaction, she could see his mind was elsewhere. Something was bothering him, something more than pondering the connection between the two deaths. It was as if he was haunted by a ghost here in Brandon, and she was pretty certain she knew who it was—it had to be his father.

Everywhere Kevin went, the man walked just ahead of him, along the streets, in the shops, entering and leaving wherever Kevin visited. He was just one step ahead of his son, leaving deep tracks behind—deep enough for Kevin to trip over, fall into. Kevin wasn't just investigating his murder—he was investigating his father because he was such an enigma. He was trying to find out who the man was who raised him and then ignored his existence once he left for New York. Kevin wasn't just searching for a killer, he was searching for his own history.

"Yeah," Kevin said at last, replying absentmindedly to her earlier remark about the prints leading to the murderer. "So, are you running around with me today?"

"Don't I always?" Margaret nodded.

Roused by the distinctive ring of his cell phone, David rolled over on the bed to grab it from the nightstand. It wasn't there. He cursed, remembering that it was on the edge of the dresser. He rolled over in the other direction, snatched it up and held it to his ear. "Yes?"

"It's John Paulin, assistant to the medical examiner," the voice on the other end stammered.

"Oh yeah, I remember you—I gave you a hundred for information on that jewelry cadaver guy."

"Yes, that's me."

"So, what's up?"

"Well, I have proof that your vic—is it cool to call a victim a vic?"

"Get on with it, John," David said, starting to lose patience.

"Oh, alright... apparently the vic—Trip Hepner—was beaten to death with a lamp base. He had a lot of bruising and torn skin on his legs and thighs, and some phalanges on both hands were broken. He received blows to the chest, back, and finally, the head."

"So, first he was beaten all over?"

"Yes. The blows to his arms and hands were most likely defensive wounds. But those around the chest and legs make it appear that he suffered a lot of pain before he was finally killed by a hard whack across the rear left quadrant of his skull and—"

Silence ensued.

"You've got something more to say, Paulin?" David said brusquely. He didn't enjoy being kept in suspense.

"I have someone on the phone who wants to speak to you. Hold on, he's on another extension."

"Who is it?"

"It's me, Mr. Allerton—Cappers from the C.S.I team. I've got a positive ID on the latents that we pulled off the lamp base."

"How did you get them so fast?" Fully alert now, David sat up in bed.

"We pulled four sets of really clear prints, and then did what we thought made the most sense, which was to pull those of the nine felons we have on record at the precinct. The second fingerprint record was the Ace of Jacks. They belong to William Hamilton, 455 Pearl Street, just outside of Brandon."

"DAMN! That's great work. Did anyone notify Chief Carville yet?" David asked with a sinking feeling.

"Oh yeah, he's already on his way to Hamilton's house."

David thanked Cappers and added, "I'll get right on this, too."

"Happy hunting, Mr. Allerton," said two voices, as Paulin chimed in with Cappers.

David slid off the bed as he dialed Kevin immediately.

Kevin's cell phone rang while he and Margaret were still at the diner. When he saw that the caller was David, he answered right away.

"Buddy, the Hepner case has been blown sky high. Carville and his band of misfits are heading to 455 Pearl Street, just outside of Brandon, to apprehend one William Hamilton. His prints were found all over the murder weapon."

"So they got him," Kevin said with a sense of relief.

"Yup, they got him, buddy. It'll take me a few minutes to get ready, but you should be there pronto since you're already mobile."

"Okay—see you at Pearl Street."

"Pearl Street," Margaret said, looking up from her plate. "What's at Pearl Street?"

"The guy who killed the jeweler." Kevin rooted around in his wallet for three twenty dollar bills and tossed them on the table. "Chief Carville is heading there now, and so is David."

"What's the hurry?!" Margaret exclaimed, wiping her lips with her napkin, before she gathered up her things to leave.

"I want to be there when they nab the murderer."

"What about David? Why can't he go without you?"

"For one thing, I have the car," he explained. "He'll

probably get there by cab, but he'll need a ride back. Plus, this death might be connected with my father's, which is why we're investigating it *together*—as you already know."

Once outside the restaurant, Kevin rushed over to the car, with Margaret skittering along behind him in her high heels. "Sonofabitch, Kevin! I'll get you for this."

In the center of a wide clearing surrounded by a tightly packed circle of White Ash and American Basswood trees were the remains of the trailer home. The branches closest to the wreckage were charred and broken. Kevin turned into a nearby grassy area that was the makeshift parking lot, where a large number of vehicles were packed tightly together. He found a vacant spot at the very edge of the lot. "You wait here," he said to Margaret.

"Why can't I come with you?"

"There might be bloodied and mutilated bodies."

"In that case, I'll stay right here." She rested her purse on her lap and reached over to turn on the radio.

"I'll be right back, baby," Kevin promised as he exited the car and strode over to a group of men standing close to the burnt-out rubble that constituted the building's remains.

The men continued talking as he approached, but their conversation stopped once the sound of crunching debris reached their ears. One of them turned around to scowl at the newcomer, but when he saw it was Kevin, he smiled broadly.

"Kevin Whitehouse! How are you doing today?" It was Harold Klein, the town's lawyer. He stretched out a hand and shook Kevin's vigorously.

Kevin found the smell of his cologne overpowering, despite the acrid stink in the air left by the fire. "I'm doing okay. But what happened here, Harold?"

"An explosion, my friend," Klein said as he returned to the group, stepping aside to make room for Kevin.

"I take it that this is—or rather, was—455 Pearl Street," Kevin said.

"Yeah, Willie Hamilton lived here," said one of the men he didn't know.

"Where is he now?"

"Dunno, the fire chief is over there," the man said as he pointed a little way off in the distance. "The cops aren't letting us get too close."

"Because it's still a crime scene," Kevin said as he walked toward the clique of firefighters. They were dressed in heavy black slickers and huge black helmets, and were scanning the immediate area around the burnt-out husk of the trailer. The Rutland fire chief, Roger Kawamura, spotted Kevin as he walked under the yellow crime scene tape.

"Whitehouse," he said. "What brings you here?"

"Chief Kawamura, how's it going? What happened here, anyway?" Kevin replied, ignoring his question.

"Well, it looks like someone wanted William Hamilton dead."

"He's dead?"

"The forensic guys are in there now going over the body with the photographer. They'll truck him down to Rutland in a few hours. After that we should get a positive ID."

Kevin looked around. "How did he die?"

"Well, I'm no detective, but from what I can tell from a

superficial examination of the crime scene, someone got to the gas line that leads to the kitchen stove, screwed it loose, and pushed it into the kitchen window. We found a large hole in the floor of the trailer near the doorway, which looks suspiciously like an explosion crater. So our first hunch that the killer was waiting somewhere outside for Hamilton to enter the trailer before setting the blaze doesn't work."

"So now, what *is* the going hunch?"

"Talk to the chief—he's over there." Kawamura indicated Carville, who was standing several yards away, possibly near the gas line's site of origin.

"Thanks, guy." Kevin clapped Kawamura on the shoulder before heading over to Carville.

"Well, *High-Powered*, what do you want?" Carville said with his back to Kevin. He must have noticed him earlier, unless he possessed some special power that enabled him to intuit Kevin's presence. In any case, he didn't wait for his approach, but instead made off in the direction of the parked cars. "I'm a busy bastard here."

Kevin followed, navigating the debris, the splintered posts, melted siding, and bits of shingles that were lying in puddles of water. "I want to know what happened."

Carville picked his own way through the debris field to a Ford truck twisted up against a tree, the back of its cab misshapen and scorched black, its windows shattered.

"What happened here?" Kevin asked. He walked past Carville to take a closer look at the vehicle.

"No one here has any skill in forensic demolitions—"

"—so you called Rutland for help."

"Yes. But from what I see, it appears that a fragmentation

grenade exploded back there," Carville said, pushing his hat back from his forehead with one hand, as he pointed to the truck bed with the other.

"Really?" Kevin said with genuine surprise, as he came around to the driver's-side door that hung open from one hinge.

"I'm no expert but it looks like it to me."

The seat backs were shredded, the stuffing sticking to the blood that was splattered everywhere inside the cab. There was also a large quantity of blood smeared down the side of the seat to the ground, where the blood trail continued raggedly along a path of loose dirt and grass leading to the trailer.

Kevin pointed down at the evidence. "Someone was dragged from the crash."

"Yeah, I know," Carville said. "Judging from the direction of the blood trail, we think it belongs to the body in the house—Willie."

"So the house was already full of gas..." Kevin mused aloud.

"Maybe yes, maybe no. One thing is for certain, Willie tried to get away, until kaboom!—the grenade exploded his truck. From there, he was dragged into his home, the killer put the gas line in, let the trailer fill with gas and then tossed in another grenade."

"So there goes our murder suspect."

"You can say that again," Carville said as he looked hard at Kevin. "I thought you two guys were such high-powered investigators, so that we could avoid more murders. All you've come up with is whatever we've come up with."

"We go where the evidence takes us," Kevin remarked with a shrug.

"Can you catch this guy?"

"We can, but only if he slips up—and since he's on the run, he'll slip up."

"I called your captain Jefferies again, to make sure about you guys, and he said there are special circumstances connected with the two of you, but that you're both capable of doing the job. I'd like you to elaborate on that, because he wouldn't."

"I honestly don't know what Jefferies is talking about. What else did he say?"

"To give you time. But I'll be forced to call the FBI if I don't get any breakthroughs soon. We're short on manpower and Rutland is beginning to complain about our dependence on them."

"I'm sorry to hear that," Kevin said sympathetically, "and you can count on us to do our best to help."

Carville sighed before he headed off to where his squad car was parked. Kevin watched him leave and noticed that the lot was beginning to empty. He was surprised to see Kawamura's red station wagon among the vehicles exiting the parking area. Kevin decided it was time for him to leave, too—especially since there were no officials left for him to interview about the crime scene. When he headed over to his car, Kevin found David leaning against the passenger side and Margaret sitting on the hood.

"So what did you find out?" David asked, holding his hand up to shade his eyes from the noon rays of the sun.

"The corpse of William Hamilton, the man whose

fingerprints are all over the weapon used to bludgeon Trip Hepner to death, is most likely back there, burnt to a crisp."

"Did he die in the fire or was he killed beforehand?" Margaret asked.

"We don't know for sure right now. It could have happened anywhere between a fragmentation grenade in his truck and the house explosion."

"More explosions," David grumbled. "Who runs around with a hand grenade in his pocket?"

"Or makes it a habit to blow up buildings?" Kevin said. Then, to David, "Didn't I tell you that my father did not kill himself?"

"It definitely smells like murder to me now," David admitted, sounding apologetic.

"But who would want to murder your father?" Margaret asked.

"I don't know yet. I'll have to deconstruct his life to get to the bottom of this."

David turned to Margaret. "How about you do the same for the jeweler?"

She smirked. "Since when do you give orders around here, David? Why don't you do it?"

"I'm going to dig into the charcoal briquette's life, over there," David said, nodding his head toward the trailer. "So, why don't you do something useful and investigate the jeweler?"

She slipped off the car, opened the passenger side door and took a seat inside.

"I don't think she likes me," David said to Kevin with a grin.

"You need to stop calling her things like 'smelly chicken-head.' "

"Can I ask you a fair question?"

"Yeah, buddy, go ahead."

"We're a team here, right?"

Kevin nodded.

"You know, Starsky and Hutch, Sherlock Holmes and Watson, McGarrett and Danno, Jake and Elwood Blues... they were all teams. They didn't have a third wheel fucking things up. I can't think of one thing that she does except bitch and moan and slow you down. Don't you want to solve your father's murder?"

"She's my fiancée, David. You need to respect that. We'll solve this. I know we will."

"You know, I liked it better when you were dating that little hotshot Asian M.E. in New York. At least you could talk shop. Whatever happened to her, anyway?"

"We just didn't see eye to eye. Too little in common."

"I see," David said as he climbed into the backseat of the car. "Could you be a pal and drop me off at the library?"

"Me, too," said Margaret. "It's as good as place as any to start investigating the jeweler. Oh, and just to be clear, David, I'm doing it for Kevin—not because *you* told me to."

David just shrugged.

"What are you looking for?" Paul Whitehouse said as he stepped through the doorway of his Uncle Richard's house.

"Paperwork," Kevin said as he swung his penlight on the end of his keychain around in the dimly lit room and found the fuse box against the wall.

"What kind of paperwork?"

"Paperwork that proves your uncle didn't kill himself." Kevin opened the fuse box and began flipping switches slowly. Soon, the comfortable yellow glow of tungsten lights brightened every corner and corridor of the rustic interior. "I think I just hit the jackpot," Kevin added.

Paul stood in the center of the foyer, looking about him cautiously, as if ghosts lurked in the remote recesses of the eerily quiet home.

"Do you know where your uncle kept all his bills and stuff, Paulie?"

Paul pointed to the right and headed toward the den. "Follow me, it's this way."

The spacious room included a large mahogany desk and wooden file cabinets, as well as wall-to-wall bookcases whose contents were askew. A conspicuous crack in the wall above one set of file cabinets continued along the ceiling, stopping at the base of the ceiling fan-light fixture combo overhead. Plaster powder covered the surfaces like a thin layer of pale dust. A few chairs were overturned, as well as some of the smaller objects like pens and pencils that were now scattered over the floor.

As he took in the scene, Kevin wondered if the house was still structurally sound. If it was, he was certain that he could convince his uncle to turn it over quickly for the first reasonable offer. He didn't want the house—he didn't even want the money. He just wanted it gone, like the rest of his life here in Brandon. For Kevin, there was nothing left, and it had been that way for some time. Even when his father was alive, there was nothing to come back for. Yes, there were *things*, old photos, and other memorabilia—as well as memories, of course—but that was all; and for Kevin, that wasn't enough. Ironically, his father's murder and funeral was the only worthwhile reason to return to Brandon.

Kevin roused himself from his reverie, and stepped over to the desk. He pulled the high-backed leather chair out, and slapped away the dust before he sat down. Then he reached into his jacket pocket and produced his reading glasses, and started with the papers on his right, making a neat stack before thumbing through them.

"What do you want me to do, Kev?" Paul asked as he paced around the room, occasionally taking down a volume and paging through it, then returning it carefully to an empty slot in the row of books.

"Do whatever you want, just stay within earshot of me."

"Okay," he said resignedly.

When they'd arrived at the library, David had followed politely behind Margaret as she went up to the reception desk to talk with a librarian. He heard her ask to use a computer with Internet access, but after that her voice trailed off and he didn't hear the rest of what she said. All he knew was that her request was granted right away, while he, on the other hand, was told he'd have to add his name to a waiting list of people who wanted to use the computers. It was a mystery to him how Margaret magically rose to the top of that list.

The Brandon public library wasn't much more than a small, well-appointed storefront tidily furnished inside with tables and chairs, and rows of bookshelves lining every wall. David sat quietly at a table along with a few locals, patiently waiting his turn. He had plenty of time to study them: they looked like simple people, with their placid, even carefree demeanors, mostly mothers with their children, and old men reading newspapers.

When his name was called, David strode over to the library's computer center. He stopped short in the middle of an aisle when he realized that all the spots at the roomier adult stations were taken. The only ones available were in the children's section, furnished with diminutive desks and chairs. Annoyed but undeterred, David took a seat at one of those. Hunched over the table, he started typing on the keyboard with two fingers.

David never considered himself the analytical member of the team—analysis was Kevin's forte. He, on the other hand, had to have things spelled out for him. For example, he liked it when he was given something specific like a name or place to deal with—something simple and finite. His first search was easy. He typed in the name William Hamilton, which brought up a long list of that name from all over the country. Then he narrowed the search to Vermont. The one William Hamilton of Vermont—who came up immediately—had a checkered past, to say the least. In several articles from local papers, he was accused of petty larceny, misdemeanors, and several felonies. Some just cost him fines, others resulted in jail time. He was a low-level thief, an aspiring smash-and-grab expert, and a crowbar was the most sophisticated tool he'd ever wielded.

Hamilton's life of crime read like a comic book. He could be depended upon to snatch a woman's purse in broad daylight when plenty of witnesses were around, or be caught fleeing a residence after setting off the burglar alarm in the course of trying to gain access. In other words, he seemed to be more of a threat to himself than to anyone else. David chuckled to himself as he went from one comedy of errors to the next, until he came to one fascinating sidebar in Hamilton's bio.

Three years ago, "Willie"—which David learned was his nickname—had been apprehended as a suspect in a bank robbery and taken in for questioning. A small savings bank in Shelburne, Vermont, about eighty miles from Brandon, had an underground vault that was robbed to the tune of six million dollars' worth of conflict diamonds from Liberia. Hamilton had no alibi, claiming that he'd spent the evening with a six-pack of beer and a DVD of a horror flick. He remained a person of interest until logic dictated otherwise: the perpetrator possessed a sophisticated knowledge of explosives as well as a blueprint of the vault, two prerequisites that would be a stretch for Hamilton. He could only have been involved after the vault was blown wide open; so, if anything, he was probably just a grunt in the operation. He was finally deemed too mentally deficient to mastermind such a job.

But it seemed clear to David that Kevin's father was involved in the heist—he was the local demolitions expert. Although the evidence against him would have been largely circumstantial, he should have been a prime suspect. A diamond heist is what Richard Whitehouse and Trip Hepner have in common, David theorized, while Willie Hamilton was the piece connecting the other two.

While David printed out the articles, questions kept popping up in his mind. How does a common thug like Hamilton get hooked up with skilled criminal types for a multimillion-dollar job? Hamilton was the smash-and-grab guy, Kevin's father was the explosives expert, and Glitter-Gun was the fence. Who was left? *If* this was the team, then who was the mastermind? Who knew where and when the diamonds would be up for grabs? Glitter-Gun? He would be the one most likely.

David got up from his chair, flexed his neck to get rid of the crick caused by his cramped position, and walked over to the printer to retrieve his printouts. He wondered if he would have to frequent the town's seedier quarters to find Willie's old haunts.

Margaret had been feeling very pleased with herself at beating David to a computer by telling the librarian that she was in the midst of a medical emergency. That she had to scan the Internet asap for clues to what ailed her three-year-old son, explaining that the family pediatrician was out of town.

But now she was thoroughly engrossed in searching the Internet for information on Trip Hepner—or, Travis Martin Hepner, III, which she quickly learned was his full name. Some of the online content associated with him consisted of advertisements for his shop and his merchandise. But she was surprised to also find his name mentioned prominently in the society pages of several local newspapers: Trip and his wife were well-known socialites.

The Hepners hobnobbed with the wealthy and powerful who owned summer cottages bordering the rivers and lakes in the countryside around Brandon. Evidently, Trip knew how to exploit these lucrative connections, making sure that he and his wife were living displays of his expensive jewelry each and every time they attended an elitist function. Margaret came across many photos attesting to this strategy.

Also, he was known to specialize in custom-made creations, designed according to the unique specifications of his high society friends. From all that Margaret could glean, Hepner's business was doing well. She could find no mention of gambling debts or substance abuse or a hint of scandal of any kind.

Was it blackmail? she wondered. Or did he witness something that made him vulnerable to murder? No, being bludgeoned to death meant something else. He must have had something that the killer wanted and refused to part with it. He was in on something bad that eventually cost him his life, she decided.

Cartons already lined the wall next to the large mahogany desk in the den, as Paul marched in with more. And the minutes spent there soon turned into hours.

"Are you finding what you're looking for, Kev?" Paul asked, resting another stack of boxes on the floor near the couch.

"I don't think so, buddy. Why don't you take a break, and I'll let you know if I need any more."

"Okay," Paul said as he wiped the dust off his shirt and pants. "I think I'll make a quick run to the Kwik-Stop for some beer and potato chips. You want anything?"

Kevin looked up from the papers he was reviewing. "Your father knows that you drink beer?"

"Yeah—yeah, he does." Paul backed away to the door.

Kevin looked at him sideways, a half-grin on his face.

Paul persisted. "Do you want anything?"

"Yeah, bring me a can of suds."

Paul nodded happily, and ducked out of the den.

Returning to the task at hand, Kevin flipped a page and scanned the text as he heard Paul drive off, the car passing below a nearby window as it headed toward the road. Then he heard a voice that almost made him jump.

"Hey, partner," David said.

Startled, Kevin looked up to see David looking for some space on the sofa that wasn't occupied by boxes. Finally, he gave up and found a chair near the desk instead. He brushed off the seat and moved it closer to Kevin before sitting down.

"What'cha doin' there?"

"The most boring work imaginable," Kevin replied. "How in the world can a man turn blowing things up into a thriving business?"

"Well, if you don't mind giving me a few minutes of your time, I'd like to ask you a few questions."

Kevin set down the sheaf of papers he was holding, and asked with a sigh, "What?"

"Can you find out where your father was working on or around March 5th, 2007?"

Kevin cleared some space on the desk, then stood up and went over to the cartons lining the wall. He checked the labels until he found the one he was looking for, and placed it on the floor near his chair. He blew the loose plaster off the top before he uncovered the contents. "What was that date again?" Kevin asked.

"March 5th, 2007."

He riffled through the folders until he located one marked "March 2007." He took it out and resumed his seat behind the desk. He pushed his reading glasses further up his nose and flipped through the pages, one after the other and then back again. "No, he had no *jobs* on that date. At least, nothing that I can find here."

"Right." David smiled with relief.

"Although, wait a minute… I see he's placed a series of orders with his vendors on the first of March for several pounds of C-4 plastic explosives, hand detonators and a bunch of other stuff that reads like Greek to me."

"Are you sure that your father had no work slated for that entire week?"

"No; in fact, it doesn't look like he had anything scheduled for the entire month of March."

David leaned forward in his chair and handed Kevin the printouts of the news clippings he'd found in the library.

"What's this?" Kevin asked as he started reading them.

David sat quietly, waiting for Kevin to reach his own conclusions.

Several long moments passed.

"You think my father was involved in this?" Kevin asked, looking stunned.

"It seems pretty obvious to me. Unless there is another demolitions expert hereabouts."

"Anybody could have helped with this heist. It doesn't have to be my father," Kevin protested.

David looked sympathetic but countered, "That may be true; but as you just said, your father had no jobs during the entire month of March of that year. Nothing on record, that is."

"Maybe he simply misplaced those work orders," Kevin suggested.

"Well, you keep hoping that, Kev." David stood and headed for the door, adding, "I'm hungry. I think I'll head out for a burger."

"Wait a minute!" Kevin pointed an accusing finger at David. "You didn't come here just to drop that idea on me and leave me to ruminate over it. You've got a plan in your head and you think you know who the killer is, don't you?"

"I wouldn't go that far, partner." David stopped at the threshold of the door. "What we got here is an out-and-out criminal equipped with your father's skills who exploded a bank vault three years ago. Now the question is: how did these three jugheads get together and why were they whacked, almost within days of each other?"

"You think my father was helping this guy Hamilton?" Kevin asked in amazement.

"Look at the evidence." David strolled back into the den. "He was busy buying explosives in the same time frame, but has no client on record for the job."

Kevin was shaking his head in disbelief. "That is all circumstantial, Dave."

"Well, do you want me to keep on digging?"

Kevin paused. "Where would you go next?"

"Let's call the cards as they land face up. Your father, dead; Trip Hepner, dead; and now William Hamilton, dead. The three of them were holding hands three years ago, but now someone has gotten greedy. With three dead, there has to be four or more. If there are four, then somebody is getting ready to get the fuck out of Dodge."

"And getting out of here is not hard. You just get in your car and head up Route 7 until you see Canada," Kevin said before returning his attention to the article. "My father was in on this? What could he have been thinking?"

"Like you would know. The two of you were estranged for years."

"Well, let's look at it this way," Kevin said. "If my father helped Willie Hamilton break in and get his hands on the diamonds, I'm certain—considering Willie's IQ—he would not be the one they would leave holding the loot."

"And your father, as the demolitions guy, wouldn't be the one to safeguard the booty either. My bet is that the jeweler, who probably masterminded the scheme, stashed it."

"In his store?" Kevin asked, perplexed. "But that would be just plain stupid. He'd have to know that the police would sift through it with a fine-tooth comb if he became a person of interest."

"I doubt that Hepner was that stupid, although Willie Hamilton certainly was. No, Trip hid that money somewhere else and wasn't saying where, which is why he was beaten to death."

Kevin added, "So Hamilton beat him to death for nothing, since he himself was killed before he could find the diamonds."

"Maybe."

They were interrupted by Margaret's sudden appearance in the doorway. She took a seat in the straight-backed chair near the sofa. "How are you two geniuses doing today?"

"Em." Kevin smiled. "You take a cab here?"

"How else?"

"Well," David said. "We're doing pretty well for a pair of guys banging their heads against a wall." Then he looked around the room irritably. "Is there a bar somewhere in here?"

"Yeah, right over there," Kevin said, indicating a distant corner.

David moved off, negotiating the boxes to the bar. Kevin looked over at Margaret's clear features, her long dark hair framing her oval face, and mischievous smile. "What's going on with you?" He asked her.

"I found out that your jeweler guy, Glitter-Gun, was a big socialite up here, rubbing elbows with the high and mighty to sell his expensive merchandise."

"So he was a wheeler-dealer," Kevin said, resettling himself in his chair. He felt more relaxed with Margaret there, especially now that the subject of his father's involvement was shelved—at least temporarily.

"He and his wife thought so. Although, from the look of his storefront, he wasn't that much of a bigshot."

"But big enough to get himself killed."

Margaret smoothed the lap of her dress. "Well, at least we have Hamilton's fingerprints on the murder weapon."

"But that still leaves us with the question—who killed Hamilton?" Kevin reminded her.

"This is true."

"I think it's time for us to start reading the forensics reports." Kevin stood up and walked over to one of the windows, then flopped into a big leather armchair nearby.

"So what did you find?" Margaret asked.

"David thinks my father may have been in cahoots with a bad crowd."

"No—really? I don't believe it," she said, sounding genuinely shocked at the idea.

"Well, so far it's all circumstantial, but his untimely death seems to be a clear indicator of malfeasance."

Margaret shook off the thought. "Are you still going to the funeral tomorrow?"

"Yeah, early in the morning."

David returned to his chair, a glass of scotch in hand. "Who do you think has the diamonds?"

"A woman," Margaret said flatly.

Looking perplexed, both men turned to her.

"Why do you say that?" Kevin asked.

"Why do men rob diamonds? Because they fence so easily?" she smirked. "They do it for women. A woman has or knows where the diamonds are."

"That sounds like pretty sexist bullshit to me," David remarked sourly.

"Did you search the phone records like you planned to?" she asked, in a not very subtle attempt to change the subject.

"I did. For both Kevin's father and Glitter-Gun. I came up empty." David took a sip from his glass.

"So you didn't do Hamilton?" Margaret asked.

"Who knew about Hamilton then?" David said defensively.

"Then let's get to the phone company now," Kevin said, getting up from the chair and looking out the window at the bright afternoon sunshine.

"Wait a minute, charger! You have a funeral tomorrow. David and I can handle this," Margaret offered.

Kevin's eyes popped open wide as he turned around to face her. "You and David?"

"Yeah, what's wrong with that?" David said. "We get along nicely when we have something to do."

"Yes, Kevin, believe it or not, when it comes to an investigation, we can work together just fine," Margaret chimed in.

"Or," David said, raising an eyebrow, "she has something she wants to gripe to me about and she wants to do it without you knowing. She probably has a few ultimatums for me."

Margaret turned to him, scowling. "I have nothing of the sort, David."

David got up to go. "How did you get out here?" he asked Kevin.

"My cousin Paul drove me." Kevin got up from the easy chair and headed back to the desk.

"Okay, I'll call for a cab." David turned to Margaret. "Are you ready, my lily-white-assed princess?"

She got up from her chair, graceful as a cat, and sauntered out of the room, saying, "Yes, my coal-black-as-slate, muscled servant."

Before he left the room, David chucked the empty glass onto the couch between two boxes, then looked at Kevin, who grimaced back at him, reflecting that he felt their going off together was a bad idea.

Alone again, Kevin got up and approached the window. He watched as they walked up the rise to the gravel road which would take them to the main, paved roadway where they could wait for the radio car to come and collect them.

He hoped they'd be okay, because they were indeed the ultimate odd couple.

Theresa at the phone company welcomed David back and ushered him into the operations room, and told him to make himself comfortable there, as before. "Sit right here, Mr. Allerton," she said, leading him to a seat. "I'll retrieve the records you asked for and generate a report for you."

Margaret trailed behind them, finding a coat rack in the corner where she peeled off her light jacket and hung it carefully on a hook.

"Is there anything else you need before I go, Mr. Allerton?" Theresa asked humbly.

"Could I trouble you for two cups of dark coffee, one sugar each?" David asked.

"Oh, yes, why certainly," the woman answered obediently, turning around and leaving the room immediately.

Margaret, not liking being ignored, followed her with her gaze and gave her the stink eye as she exited.

"I wonder what *her* problem is?" Margaret asked.

"You didn't flash a badge. She appreciates men with badges and guns."

Margaret huffed, and then eased into the seat next to David.

Theresa returned with the cups of coffee, carefully resting them down next to David. "I'll be back with the reports in a few minutes."

David and Margaret chatted for a short while over coffee, speculating about Richard Whitehouse's involvement in the heist, and expressing concern about the impact it would have on Kevin if he learned his father was a criminal.

Then Theresa was back with the reports, which she handed to David. "If there's anything else you need, please feel free to call me on the phone, Mr. Allerton. Extension 223."

David turned to her, smiled, and then nodded. "Thank you. I'll call you if I need you."

Theresa smiled back, smoothed her blouse down over her breasts, then turned and left the room.

"I wonder what that's all about?" David said, sounding annoyed. Then he turned his attention to the reports, handing over half the stack to Margaret.

"Looks to me like she has a case of Jungle Fever," Margaret observed with a mischievous smile.

David chuckled. "Yeah, maybe she'd like to suck on the ol' chocolate bar."

Margaret just snorted in disgust, and changed the subject as she started perusing the phone records. "Hmm, it looks like this Hamilton guy lived on the phone."

"I know. The motherfucker has a stack of phone records printed out for every day. I wonder how he could afford it."

"Petty crimes, maybe?"

David kept scanning the pages, relaxing his eyes so that something would come together and make sense.

"Okay," Margaret said. "What I think we have to figure out is who made the most calls to his cell in a given time period. Let me include the calls from your half of the reports."

"That sounds like a plan," David said as he handed it over.

After a few minutes, Margaret said, "I've got it! Katherine Werthers, 37 South Carvers Street, Brandon, Vermont."

David mused aloud. "Who's she? A girlfriend or something?"

"Seventy-eight phone calls in one week. I doubt she's his housemaid. Should we go talk to her?"

"You and me together? I don't think that's a good idea," David replied, looking dubious.

Margaret suddenly bristled. "But what can happen with the two of us there talking to her? Not only do women tend to bond with each other, but she might be more relaxed if she's not all alone with big bad you."

David thought about this for a moment as he stood up and headed for the door. "Okay—but don't try to play cop or I'll run your narrow little ass back into the car, get me?"

"I get you. I get you." Margaret whipped out of the chair and over to the coat rack, snatching her jacket and following David out.

The entrance to Katherine Werthers' home was up a flight of stairs that ran alongside the two-family house. David rapped on the door with his knuckles, making a hollow sound, as the two stood on the narrow landing together. They waited patiently, but there were no signs of life from within.

"Knock again," Margaret suggested.

David knocked on the door again, more forcefully this time. Then he said, "Give Kevin a call."

"And tell him what?"

"Keep passing information, no-nuts. Information sharing is more vital than you know."

Margaret reached into her jacket and found her cell phone. Flipping it open, she speed-dialed Kevin and put the phone to her ear.

"Kevin!" she exclaimed, happy to hear a friendly voice. She didn't like to admit it, but David's belittling of her sometimes got her down. "We've got a lead; we just don't know where she is."

"Who's the lead?" Kevin asked.

"Katherine Werthers. She seems to be in some sort of relationship with Willie Hamilton. We need to talk to her as soon as possible."

"Okay, I'll get Carville on it right away." Then there was a pause. "You be careful. David can get into some pretty serious trouble."

"Oh, I'm sure I can handle it, sweetheart," she said before slapping her cell phone shut.

Suddenly, David reared back and drove the flat of his shoe into the door lock, shattering the bolt from the strike plate. He pushed the door aside, flicked the light switch next to it, and found himself in a hallway adjacent to a small kitchen.

"David! This is breaking and entering!" Margaret cried out in alarm.

"It's only B&E if you're a cop or a robber."

"Where in the hell did you get that idea?"

David ignored Margaret's question, and walked over to the kitchen table where there was a floral arrangement, placemats, and a pad and pencil. He picked up the pencil and then the pad, and softly rubbed the paper in search of an impression, uncovering a laundry list.

"What are you doing?" Margaret hissed, coming up behind him.

"Something I saw in the movies." He tore off the paper and shoved it into his pocket. "You look over there," David said, pointing to the living room.

"What am I looking for?" she asked.

"Anything out of the ordinary."

She moved slowly into the dimly lit room. "What would that look like? I have no idea."

David gave her no answer. Instead, he returned to the hallway to study the photographs that lined the wall: one of a young husband and wife with their toddler daughter; then another depicting the same girl, older, at her high school graduation. Next he entered the bedroom, went over to the dresser and started riffling through the drawers. David didn't know exactly what he was looking for, but he knew he'd know it if he saw it.

Margaret made a half-hearted search of the living room, looking around for anything that might qualify as "out of the ordinary," until she came to a phone perched on a table next to the loveseat. She sat down, lifted the receiver and pressed *69. She listened intently as the number of Ms. Werthers' last caller was announced by an electronic female voice, and hung up the phone. She went back to the kitchen to retrieve a piece of paper and pencil, and jotted down the number from memory. She returned to the phone in the living room and dialed the number. After three rings, the call was picked up by an answering machine.

"You have reached the home of Harold Klein. I'm not in right now, but if you'll please leave a message…"

Harold Klein opened his front door and smiled when he saw Katherine Werthers standing on the other side, dressed only in tight jeans and a flimsy white shirt despite the chilly weather. She had been staring into the dusky night sky until she heard the door open.

"Katherine," Klein said. "What brings you here at this hour?"

"Like I told you on your answering machine, I desperately need some legal advice, or any advice for that matter. Please, I have to talk to you—" Katherine's usually shiny blonde hair, cut at the jawline, was dull and shapeless. She had dark circles under her eyes and her sallow skin had a yellow pallor.

"I called you back, but you didn't answer."

"I left for here right after I left the message."

"Jeez, I hope you don't mind my saying this, but you look like shit! When was the last time you had a good night's sleep?" Klein said, as he beckoned her inside.

"I don't know… maybe two days."

"Two days? Wow! What's going on with you?" Behind his thick black-framed glasses, his eyes expressed obvious concern as he looked her up and down. After he closed the door, he turned on the hall light, causing Katherine to flinch.

"Whoa! Calm down there," he said as he slid his hand over to her waist to usher her into his living room. He pointed to one of two couches, and suggested she sit. "Let me get you something to drink to calm your nerves," he said as he left the room.

Katherine stood motionless for a few minutes near the

couch he indicated, as if wondering what the piece of furniture was for before lowering herself into it.

Harold retrieved two highball glasses and found a bottle of Merlot in the kitchen. Quickly popping the cork, he filled the glasses and returned to the living room, where he handed one to Katherine. She reached out and took it with two trembling hands, and drank a few gulps of wine immediately.

Harold grabbed a chair and swung it around, parking it in front of her. "Okay—now tell me, what's up?"

"Harold, I don't know where to begin. You wouldn't believe me if I told you."

Klein ran his fingers through his thick gray hair and sighed. "Why don't you just take another sip and start where you feel the most comfortable? I'll ask questions if I get lost."

She looked at him gratefully as she raised the glass to her lips, taking another sip before she began to talk. "It happened three years ago. I was working as a bank manager at the Franklin Savings Bank in Shelburne, and I was doing my job as usual, when a client came in, looking to put money in our bank. It was Travis Martin Hepner, III."

"Trip?"

"Yeah. Trip drops by and tells me that he wants to put a million dollars in our safe. You know, you see this guy with all the rich and famous people in the local papers and you know he's not just blowing smoke; and to land him as a client for my bank could mean a big promotion. But the fact was he was feeling me out, asking all kinds of questions while I was trying to fill out his paperwork. It soon became apparent to me that he didn't have the money. He just wanted my help." She was clearly distressed and still shaking as she raised the glass of wine to her lips to fortify herself before she continued.

"It turned out that six million dollars' worth of diamonds from Liberia was making a stopover at our bank. You see, they move these things around a lot to fool criminals or keep them at bay, but it didn't work this time. Somehow—I don't know how—Trip got the information that in two weeks the diamonds were going to be in my bank for twenty-four hours before being moved south to New York."

"He knew this?"

"Yeah, yeah," Katherine nodded decisively. "He had everything he needed to nab these diamonds except for the floor plans. He needed the architectural blueprints for the bank and the layout of the basement in the building next to it."

"Could you get them?" Harold never dreamed that someone like Katherine could have gotten involved in something as exotic as this. He leaned forward in his chair so as not to miss a word she said.

"Of course, I could. I was the bank manager. The real trick was to copy them without anyone's knowledge, which was the most important issue for Trip. No one could know. My actions had to be totally invisible."

"And when it was done?"

"I would get a check for one million, two hundred thousand."

"Jesus," Harold gasped. He turned up his glass, draining it. "I've got to get another. Do you want some more wine?"

"Yes, please." Katherine seemed more relaxed, now that she had unburdened herself to someone else, or that she had taken alcohol into her bloodstream.

Harold took her glass and headed back to the kitchen, and was back in a flash with two full glasses.

"What happened next?" he asked eagerly as he resumed his seat.

"Well, I moved cautiously. I did a little homework, found the architect, used my feminine wiles…"

"Huh?" Harold said, perplexed.

"You may think less of me after this, but I had to move fast with the architect. I didn't have time to let him woo me, so I had to have sex with him immediately. It was the only way I could get the blueprints we needed," she explained. "I got close enough to him right away so that I could gain easy access to his office. You know, meet him there for a date earlier than we'd agreed to, poke around while he was busy with clients. Finally, I was able to get them without his knowing, and after making the copies, I gave them to Trip immediately."

"And then what?"

Katherine leaned back on the couch and caught her breath before resuming her story. "A week to the day after I gave him the plans, the bank is hit and the diamonds are taken. Just the diamonds, nothing else."

"The deal went through?"

She nodded. "Two days later, Trip comes back and tells me that we have to wait five years before we get paid! I don't like the idea, you know, but who am I going to complain to? And then, I see on television that they have a person of interest for the robbery. Willie Hamilton."

"So you think Willie is a part of this deal, too?"

"I knew he was. I had that gut feeling. Months later, after

the police had dropped the charges against him, I arranged to meet him in a restaurant all the way up in Castleton where nobody we knew would see us together. I told him that I supplied the blueprints for the job. He told me he knew that already. He just happened to be dead center of the operation and knew everybody involved. He said that it was him, Trip, that Whitehouse guy, and now me.

"We began to see each other a lot, and talk about what we would do with the money we'd be getting in a few years. And then it turned sexual and our plans changed. By now three years had passed, and we were thinking that maybe three years was enough, that the diamonds would be cool enough to fence. But the idea got a real grip on Willie, much more than it did me, and he decided to push Trip hard about the money. He wanted his share and he wanted it soon. Finally, things got really ugly between them, and before you know it, this... this..."

"This what?" Harold asked, sounding frustrated.

"This Richard Whitehouse guy blows himself up."

"You think he committed suicide? Why on earth would he?"

"He got involved because Trip's plan needed a demolitions expert—and who else could he find around here? Trip thought he was perfect because everyone in Brandon loved him for the kids' fireworks show, so he'd never be a suspect. Richard Whitehouse had to live a long time with the guilt, and the waiting made him crazy, too—for the money and then with the fear of being found out. He must have gotten wind of the fact that Willie was going to stir things up. So he took the coward's way out...maybe."

"Wait a minute, the math's wrong. One million, two

hundred thousand goes into six million five times. There was only four of you."

"Yeah, I know. I never questioned it, I just assumed that Trip was keeping two fifths of the money because he was the brains behind the operation."

"Okay, so first the money was being split five ways. But with Whitehouse gone, it suddenly goes up to a million and a half for you and Willie," Harold observed.

"Yeah, now there's more at stake, and that's when Willie decides to cash in. So he moves in on Trip, demanding to know where the diamonds are, and kills him trying to find out."

"And did he find out?"

"Yes. Well, sort of."

"Sort of?"

"Trip gave him a general idea of where to find them, but it's not very specific."

"What good is a general idea?" Harold exclaimed, astounded by now at the baffling degree of stupidity in the heist's cast of characters.

"None, I guess," Katherine said, sounding defeated.

Harold thought for a moment. "First Richard Whitehouse... and then Willie Hamilton is dead. Do you know who killed him?"

"Not a clue."

Harold reasoned, "So, either Willie took the location of the diamonds with him to his grave, or he told his killer where they can be found."

"Yes—either or."

"What are you going to do?" Harold said, looking at her again with an expression of concern.

"I don't know."

"Listen, Katherine, your cohorts are dropping like flies. What you have to do is approach Carville with your story as soon as possible, just in case Willie gave up your name to his killer. He could have said you were in on the scheme, that you masterminded it, that you even know the whereabouts of the diamonds."

Katherine swallowed hard. "But I *do* know the whereabouts of the diamonds."

Harold paused as if Katherine had changed species right before his eyes. "I thought you said that Willie had only a *general* idea of their whereabouts."

"He did. Trip put him in the ballpark and Willie told me where that was."

Harold sighed, thought for a while and then looked directly into Katherine's eyes. "Whoever killed Whitehouse and Hamilton is undoubtedly after you. You *must* go to the police and tell them everything you know for your own protection."

"Do you think I'm in danger?"

"Yes, very much so, because you hold all the pieces of the puzzle—minus one. The identity of the killer!"

"I guess I didn't think it through, that Willie might have told someone about me and my part in the heist," Katherine said.

What she didn't say, she thought: How could she let herself get into such a mess? Greed? Money? Power? Like Trip, Willie had been no more than a simple conduit to a great deal of money. It had entailed some nights of rancid sex, some boozy weekends; and she'd managed to convince him that they were in love and that together they could easily get their hands on their cut of the six million dollars' worth of diamonds two years early. But now there was at least one dangerous, faceless person searching for her and the diamonds, who would do anything—including killing her—to get them.

Harold broke into her thoughts. "Listen, Katherine, we've wasted too much time as it is. Someone already knows you have information about the diamonds and they'll be coming after you for it."

"So, what do I do?"

Harold got to his feet. "We've got to get you to a safe place."

"To Carville, right?" She rose from the couch and looked at him with pleading eyes.

"Yes, Carville," he agreed.

At that moment, the doorbell rang. Both Harold and Katherine froze solid as statues.

"Who's that?" Katherine gasped, her heart pounding in her chest.

"Stay in the shadows," Harold advised, waving her off to the left.

The doorbell rang again, this time repeatedly.

"Who is it?" Harold shouted.

"It's me, Harold," Carville called out. "C'mon, open up!"

Harold breathed a sigh a relief. He went to the window first, to make sure it was him, and then unlocked the door.

Carville strode in, removing his hat. When he saw the

anxious expression on Harold's face, he said, "What's the matter with you?"

"You won't believe what I have to tell you."

"What?"

"Willie Hamilton killed Trip Hepner."

Carville sighed, "We already know that, bud." Then added, "Do you have any cold beers in the refrigerator?" Without waiting for an answer, he headed straight for the kitchen, where he found Katherine cowering behind the counter. "Katherine?" he exclaimed. "Is there something going on here that I shouldn't be privy to?"

"No, Chief. In fact, we urgently need to talk to you," she replied with an obvious measure of relief as she stood up from her crouching position.

"Okay, but can I get a beer first?" He opened the refrigerator and retrieved a cold one. "So, now, what's the story?"

Harold entered the kitchen and stood next to Katherine. "Listen, Labrec, six million dollars in conflict diamonds taken from a heist three years ago are stashed around here, and people are killing themselves over them. Katherine's life is in danger."

Carville leaned against the counter thoughtfully drinking his beer. "Oh, so that's what's going on..."

Katherine nodded frantically. "Yes. Richard Whitehouse is already dead, possibly not by his own hand, Hepner's been murdered—and now Willie Hamilton, too. I was involved, so I could be next."

Carville carefully set down his beer and pulled his two-way receiver from his belt. "I'll get the details about your part later, Katherine, but does anyone know who has the diamonds or where they're at?"

"Katherine?" Harold turned to her.

"They're supposed to be up at Trip's summer house at Lake Dunmore. He's kept them there for three years now," Katherine said.

"Where? Buried underground, or in some secret hiding place inside the house?" Carville asked.

"I swear I don't know," Katherine replied. "I just know that the diamonds are up there *somewhere*."

"That's going to mean a pretty big search grid," Harold said.

Addressing Katherine, Carville asked, "Don't you have any specifics at all? A certain room, a wall safe—anything?"

She shook her head ruefully. "Hepner told Willie. I was outside, waiting in the truck. So all I know is what Willie told me."

There was a pause as Carville put his transceiver back, and picked up his beer from the counter.

Katherine turned to Harold then, who just stared back at her blankly.

"So..." she began, her gaze on the police chief now. "What are we going to do? Are you going to call in a bunch of deputies to help us dig around the shore house and find those diamonds?"

"Don't have enough deputies for that," Carville said with a grimace. "Besides, they'll all want a cut."

Katherine was stunned, and shook her head in disbelief. "Want a cut? What are you talking about?" she asked incredulously.

Then there was a dull thump and Katherine staggered. She looked around for the source and found Harold pointing the silenced end of a shiny black Walther PPK at her, its muzzle smoldering.

"What the fuck is going on here?" she managed to whisper through her abject terror, groping her blouse and finding a bullet hole ringed with blood. Unbelievable as it was, she'd been shot.

"Stupid bitch," Harold said angrily. "While you were busy spreading your legs for every nickel and dime you thought you'd be getting, we were doing the real fucking work." He raised the gun again and fired into her belly, the impact this time knocking her to the floor.

"Who do you think told Trip about the diamonds? The Liberian client was mine. He was going to fence the diamonds in five years if we could keep them away from the Feds. The client tells me, I tell Trip, and Trip gets the crew. But Labrec and I had no intention of splitting the money six ways. We were going to wait out the five years, cash in the diamonds and then disappear. I just told Trip that there would be a five-way split just to get you bunch of hillbillies to do the job."

Katherine didn't speak or move, she didn't have the strength. The blood was spilling out of her along with what was left of her life.

Harold persisted, as if impelled by an outside force to disclose all before she died. "Then your asshole boyfriend Willie got himself implicated in the heist. Which is when it was a good idea to have the chief in on the deal." Harold gestured with his head to Carville. "My friend here was skillful enough to fade the heat, turn away suspicion, and have the case against Willie dropped."

Finished with his story, Harold lifted up the gun and fired at Katherine one last time. Now she was dead.

"Fucking greedy fools," Carville remarked as he turned around to the refrigerator to get himself another beer. "Because of them we have to figure out where the diamonds are hidden, when they would have just plopped into our hands in another two years."

"Well, what's done is done. Nothing we can do about it." Harold stepped over to Katherine's body where it lay in a puddle of blood. Her head was thrown back, her mouth was agape, and her eyes were wide open, staring unseeing at the ceiling.

"Why the fuck did I kill her in my own kitchen?" Harold wondered aloud, shaking his head in exasperation. "This is going to be a bitch to clean up."

"You did it because you're an asshole."

"I'm an asshole? No, you're an asshole."

"Now, what the hell are *we* doing?" Carville said, holding the fresh bottle of beer in hand. "We're just wasting precious time that could be spent finding those diamonds."

"Well then, you'd better get your ass in gear pronto so you can get up to Lake Dunmore and search the premises of Hepner's home. Maybe we'll get lucky," Harold suggested. "And just remember, my friend, without me and my client, those diamonds are worthless to you."

Carville tilted the bottle up, drained it quickly, and let out a loud burp when he was done. "Okay, boss. I'm off."

"We're heading over to Harold Klein's home right now," Margaret said into her cell phone.

"Wait for me. I'm taking a cab up there right now!" Kevin implored.

"We're almost there. You'd just be slowing us down."

"Slowing *us* down! When did you become part of an *us*?"

"You know what I mean."

"I'll take care of her, Kev," David shouted at the phone, while keeping his eyes on the dark road ahead. "Just like I take care of you."

"Very funny, dickhead! I don't like this. I'm coming up anyway."

Then Margaret heard only silence on the line.

"Hung up, did he?" David asked, as he negotiated a turn with the tires wailing.

"He's being overprotective."

"Like you?"

She thought about the comment for a moment. "I guess I am a little overprotective. But I know he has an ex-Special Forces operative with him and that makes me feel better."

"But you like the rush now, don't you?"

"It's compelling," Margaret admitted.

"Well, this is how it's going down. I'll go in alone to do some questioning. You stay in the car."

"Why? Why is that?" she asked him angrily.

Ignoring her question, David mused aloud. "Something seems fishy here. Katherine Werthers gets in contact with the town lawyer after her boyfriend is blown to bits? Why not the police chief, if she has something to tell?"

"Well, Klein did call her, but we don't know if she reached

out to him. Also, maybe his call was just to return hers. We don't know that either."

"Okay. Let's agree that she went to Klein's house, for reasons unknown."

"Maybe she wants to see what legal recourse she has before incriminating herself by going to the police," Margaret reasoned.

"That's actually a very sensible theory. But it means they'll be shooting me in the foot with the attorney-client privilege bit, which doesn't make me too happy."

"So, what do you plan to do?"

"Break some fucking skulls in," David said with relish.

"You can't do that! You're a cop."

"I'm a..." David paused. "I'm no longer on the force. I'm a disabled detective and an assistant town deputy. That sounds like a long way from cop to me."

Margaret shook her head resignedly, and turned to stare out of the window.

"Have you ever fired a shotgun before, Margaret?"

"No, oh, no."

"Gotta make it a smaller gun then." David ducked low, his eyes at the same level as the top of the steering wheel. "That's the driveway there."

David killed the lights and pulled the car to a stop along the curb in front of Klein's house. He climbed out of the car and went around to the trunk with Margaret following him. When he opened it, she saw four leather rifle bags.

"Guns?" she exclaimed.

"No. Lollipops, baby." David reached in, unzipped one

and laid it flat, exposing three handguns, and a long rifle with magazines, and a telescopic sight.

Margaret stood by, speculating silently on what all this meant—and what might come next. It was dark, it was night, and David was fully armed. There was something in the pit of her stomach that assured her that this was not going to end well.

"Hmm… something light," David muttered to himself. Then he pointed to a handgun just slightly larger than the palm of his hand. He picked it up and handed it to her. "Now, how heavy is that?" he asked her.

She took the gun and passed it from hand to hand, nodding. "It's pretty light."

"Beautiful. It's a Sig Sauer P238. It'll give anyone with the intention of harming you another agenda."

"Is it loaded?" Margaret said, holding the gun more carefully.

David took the gun, reached into the bag and pulled out a magazine. He slapped it into place, worked the slide, then flicked the safety on.

"See this lever?" he said, pointing to it.

Margaret moved her eyes in close and nodded.

He flicked it. "When you see that red dot, she's ready to fire. That's your safety."

"Safety," she repeated.

David flicked the safety back and dug into another bag, this time producing a stubby fourteen-inch Remington Model 870P shotgun with a modified barrel. There was no shoulder stock on the weapon, so he hooked a looped strap at the end of it and slung it over an arm. Finally, he snatched up a simple Glock 19 and shoved it into his pants, behind his belt.

"What's the plan?" Margaret whispered.

"I'm pretty good at this shit alone. If you see anyone run out of the house and it's not me, shoot at them, man or woman. Try to kill them since with your skill you'll only scare or graze them."

"Is that supposed to be funny?"

David returned to the driver's side of the car and motioned for Margaret to get comfortable inside.

Clearly annoyed, Margaret did his bidding; she settled herself on the passenger side and slammed the door shut.

David shook his head at her carelessness. How could she be so oblivious to their surroundings? Didn't she know that making a loud sound at such a moment could immediately expose them to danger? Which is exactly why she needed to stay in the car.

David crouched down and moved stealthily up the driveway of Klein's home until he came to a tree he could duck behind. Then he followed the shadow of the tree as he got closer to the house, leading him to the rear, where he had a clear view through the open windows—which, fortunately, were well lit from inside. As far as he could tell, that part of the house was empty.

Close to his position was an open garage, where two cars were parked. He crouched behind the first vehicle, a Ford Focus, and found the exhaust pipe cool to the touch. He crept to the back of the next car, a Volkswagen Golf; its tailpipe was considerably warmer. David figured Klein had company, a relatively new arrival.

He moved deeper into the garage, finding the door to

the house behind an iron gate. He glanced over his shoulder before he pulled a lock pick from his jacket and made short shrift of the cheap gate lock. The lock on the door gave him a little more trouble, but after a few moments more, he heard the bolt slide back from the strike plate. He turned the door-knob very slowly and peeked inside. The door opened onto an area between the kitchen and the dining room.

David decided to enter the dining room first. He found it dark and apparently uninhabited. While he was looking around, he thought he heard a noise emanating from the kitchen. He headed in that direction until he encountered the dead body of a young woman sprawled on the floor, blood puddling everywhere from beneath it. His first thought was that it had to be Katherine Werthers.

Unperturbed, David slung the snub-nosed shotgun into his hands and crouched low. He moved a few steps forward before he saw a man—his back to him—holding a spray bot-tle of bleach in one hand and a large sponge in the other.

"Doing some late-night cleaning?" David casually inquired.

Howard Klein spun around so fast that he slipped and fell back against the counter. He stared in shock and disbe-lief at David, who stood calmly before him, pointing a shot-gun in his direction.

"Kevin Whitehouse!" Klein gasped.

"Nope. You got us mixed up, buddy. I'm David."

Klein blinked and frowned in utter confusion. This was Kevin Whitehouse, wasn't it? Or maybe his name wasn't Kevin Whitehouse to begin with?

"Okay, uh... David, then. Wha... what are you doing here?" Klein, nonplussed by the sudden turn of events, could barely get the words out, he being caught with a body on his kitchen floor.

"You don't ask the questions, I do." David shook the gun barrel at him. "Now think about this before you answer and you'll have a nicer day. Who's the bloody corpse on the floor?"

"Katherine Werthers."

"Why'd you kill her?"

Klein grimaced. Then he remembered that on the counter to his right was the Walther PPK with a few rounds still in the magazine. It would take only a moment's distraction to get his hands on it.

"You're a second away from having your blood mingle with hers on the floor there."

"She knew too much."

"Like about the conflict diamonds?"

Harold nodded.

"So here we got a bunch of dysfunctional children out to make an easy buck knocking each other off. To summarize, you killed Katherine Werthers, Willie Hamilton killed Trip Hepner. My question to you is: Who killed Richard Whitehouse and Willie Hamilton? Your partner?"

"I don't have a partner."

"Is it just because I'm from New York you think I'm stupid? You *have* to have a partner, the body count is too high. You want me to believe that you are capable of killing off a trained demolitions expert and a tough-as-nails felon? No, you're a pussy. You, it's clear that you can kill women, but I doubt men. That's why I know you have a partner. Now where is he?"

Harold thought carefully about the question. He hadn't given the murder of Willie much thought. Whitehouse was no doubt a suicide, but Willie was murdered. Could it have been Carville? Or was there another player in the game that even he didn't know about. One thing for certain was the shotgun pointing at him. He looked at the wide barrel, and the more he did, the harder his heart pounded.

"I… I'm not a pussy," was the only reply he could come up with.

"You must realize that the show is over for you," David said, lowering the muzzle of the gun slightly. "The next ride for you, unless you can make me as dead as that woman there, is a long time in prison. Now you can let your partner get to the diamonds and live out the rest of his life in some tropical paradise living like a king, or you can help me nab him for the murders of Whitehouse and Hamilton."

"I have nothing to say to you."

"Here's a thought for you as you rot in jail for the rest of your life, getting your asshole examined by every con in your cell block. What if I received an anonymous call to my cell to come to your house and look around? Did that same person tell you to shoot her? Or did you think you were taking the initiative in killing her and staining only your own hands with blood?

"What are you talking about?"

"Your partner turned you in. He gave you up. You get caught red-handed and take the rap, while he buys enough time to get to the diamonds and leave the country." David smiled. "Not only are you a pussy, you're a patsy too. You're new at this, aren't you?"

"Shut up."

"Fine by me. He gets a pass, you go to prison."

"So be it."

"But, you don't get to go to prison without a considerable number of bumps and bruises along the way—like falling on the floor and bumping into the nearby furniture."

"Are you threatening me, officer?"

"Oh, yes, very much so. I'm going to beat on you until you tell me what you know; and you'll give it up gladly, knowing that your scumbag friend doesn't get to go on holiday while you die in lockup."

"You can't do anything to me—you're a cop."

"I'm a cop on disability. You don't see any guns on me, do you?" David held up the shotgun in one hand and opened his jacket with the other, showing off the Glock butt tucked behind his front belt. "Do you understand me?" He moved in on Harold, eyes locked on his as he said, "Who is he?"

Harold suddenly raised the bottle and sprayed him liberally in the face with the bleach.

Stunned, David coughed and grimaced, shutting his eyes tightly. He was blinded, but still able to hear the sound of something heavy being snatched off the counter nearby.

Harold had made a desperate lunge to grab the Walther, then turned around, gun arm outstretched, aiming for David's chest.

But David was ready for him. Still holding his shotgun by the shortened stock, he flipped it in his hand catching the barrel, cocked it back and swung the end of it like a baseball bat, smashing the shotgun end across Harold's jaw with a crack. The blow sent him sprawling to the floor, spitting blood and teeth.

David flung away the shotgun, staggered to where he remembered the sink to be, and turned on the cold water full force. He then proceeded to splash it vigorously into his eyes and mouth.

Harold lay stunned on the spot where he had fallen, his ears ringing, the room spinning around him so fast he thought he would vomit. Finally, he managed to raise himself up on his hands to glance around for the Walther. The effort was futile—not only was he dizzy, he was now without his glasses.

Knowing time was of the essence, Harold quickly gave up on the gun and groped for the counter, using it to gain his footing. Then he staggered out of the kitchen and made his way to the garage door, yanking it open and shouldering the gate in front of him aside. Could he drive like this? he wondered, as he stepped toward the Ford Focus. It was then that he was struck on the head from behind. The ground rushed up at him and swallowed him into a dark abyss.

Harold woke up on the kitchen floor, face down, the back of his head bleeding. The first thing he did was stick two fingers in his mouth to discover that three teeth were missing. Next he attempted to climb to his knees, but found his ankles tied together.

"Shit," he groaned.

Then David stood before him, but Harold could only see his shoes.

"Hey, buddy," David cooed. "Do you remember me? The guy you were trying to blind?"

In response, Harold moaned in pain.

"I was lucky it was a water and bleach solution, wasn't I?"

"What do you want?" Harold growled. "I know my rights. I want to speak to my lawyer. I want to be taken in."

"No, that's not going to happen, buddy. Not tonight. First, I'm going to stage the crime scene a little."

"Stage?"

"Yeah, that's when I move the dead bodies around like Ken and Barbie dolls to make it match my own scenario."

"You can't do that," he snarled.

David kicked him hard on the tip of his nose, causing him to yelp and roll over onto his back. "I guess I can't do that either."

"What do you want!" Harold held his face, shouting, his nose now running with blood.

"Who's your partner and where did he go for the diamonds?"

Just then, David heard the front door open. He took a cautious step away from Harold, holding up the police shotgun as he headed toward the living room. There he found Kevin and Margaret standing together, peering silently around the room. David gave them a quick nod to indicate that everything was okay.

Returning to Harold, David knelt low. "You've already got one murder on your hands—for sure. And I'm tired of giving you chances. So, for the last time, who's your partner and where is he now?"

Harold simmered with pain and anger and frustration, but said nothing.

"You think I'm kidding you?"

Harold did not reply.

"Well, Harold, as you know, all the world's a stage!" With a grand flourish, David grabbed Harold by his bound ankles and dragged him across the kitchen floor, through the short hall and into the living room.

"OKAY! OKAY!" Harold protested. "Okay, I'll tell you!"

"Speak up then—time's a-wasting."

"Katherine told us that the diamonds were somewhere up at Trip's beach house."

"Who's working with you?"

"Carville."

"Carville killed Richard Whitehouse and Willie Hamilton?"

"I swear I don't know. All I know is that he's up there now, rooting around, looking for the diamonds."

David turned to Kevin and Margaret, who were standing nearby.

"So?" Kevin asked David. "What do you want to do?"

"We can't call the deputy in on this…" David said, stepping away from Harold, who lay in a near fetal position at his feet.

"We can call Rutland PD, explain about Carville and have them send up their men. Meanwhile, you stay here while I go up to the beach house and catch him in the act," Kevin suggested.

"Oh, no," David said emphatically.

"You've got to be kidding, Kevin," Margaret said. "That's absolutely way too dangerous!"

"I can handle it, Margaret."

"Like hell you can."

David nodded. "One thing is for certain. We have to call this in, especially if Carville has already gotten his hands on the loot and tries to leave the state—even the country, for that matter. If we move fast to get a jump on him, it could make all the difference."

"So you're calling it in?" Kevin asked.

"Yeah," David said, pulling out his smartphone. "Remember, you've got a funeral in the morning. I'll tip off Rutland tonight and get them involved, and tomorrow afternoon we'll hit the beach house and see what kind of evidence we can find there."

The wisdom of David's words wasn't lost on Kevin, who nodded tiredly. "You can keep the car since you don't know how long you'll need to be here. We'll get a cab back home."

David turned to Harold. "Keep your ass still. If I come back in here and find that you've moved one iota, I'll hurt you some more."

"Yeah, yeah," Harold groaned, feeling new pain in the bloodied back of his head.

David accompanied Kevin and Margaret to the front door, remaining alert to Harold's presence behind him.

"Good luck with that," Kevin said to David, nodding in Klein's direction, as he followed Margaret outside.

The minute the door closed behind them, David went back to Harold and stood over him while he called 911 on his cell.

"911—do you need police, fire or ambulance?" inquired a female voice on the other end.

"Please connect me to the Rutland police department," David said.

"Hold on, sir."

"Rutland police department."

"Yeah, Rutland PD. I have some very serious charges to file against a local law enforcement official, so I need a department outside of Brandon's jurisdiction," David said.

"Please hold," the voice said.

David, restless, headed back to the front of the house and peeked out the window at Kevin and Margaret as they waited for the cab. He thought they did make a lovely couple, even if she was such a fucking chickenhead.

The driveway and street outside Klein's house were packed with cars and an ambulance from the Rutland police department, who brought their forensic crew, photographers and other personnel. David was sitting just inside the open rear doors of an ambulance parked in the driveway, being administered to by two paramedics for the injuries he suffered from the bleach. They treated him for minor burns around his eyes, gave him a nasal spray for the irritation to his nostrils, as well as some salve for his lips.

After he'd been fussed over enough, David waved them away and left the ambulance, crossing the lawn to go back inside. There he found a busy hub of activity, with photographers clustered around the corpse and members of the forensics team roaming the house. As he walked down the hall from the kitchen, David encountered a tall, well-built young man wearing a cowboy hat and tan-colored uniform. He stopped when he saw David, effectively blocking his path; then he snatched off his hat and stuck out his hand.

"Are you David Allerton?" he asked.

David shook his hand vigorously. "Yes, I am."

"I'm Rutland's sheriff, Dale Cummings. I'm glad to see that you're okay."

"Yeah, I'm alright. My eyes and nose are a little sensitive, but otherwise I'm fine."

Cummings held his hat in two hands before him and rocked on his heels. "How in the world did you manage to catch this guy in the act?"

"A number on the victim's caller ID brought me here. And then, like they say, timing is everything."

"What happened when Klein saw you?"

"When I identified myself as a deputy of the law, he raised his hands and acted like he was going to surrender. But before I knew it, he sprayed me with some bleach cleaner he was already holding in his hand—getting ready to clean up the crime scene, you know."

Cummings put his hat back on his head, reached into his back pocket and pulled out a pad. Flipping it open, he began to write. "Then what?"

"I went on Brooklyn automatic and fucked him up."

"Brooklyn automatic," Cummings laughed. "I can see that. You also said that he implicated Carville in a bank heist and the murder of at least two people you know of."

"Yes, Klein implicated Chief Carville." David paused, perplexed. "Where is Klein, anyway? Isn't he talking to you?"

"He's in the dining room. He's talking alright; I just wanted to get your version of what happened."

"Yeah, I understand." David nodded.

"We'll get a judge on this right away—have Carville apprehended and suspended as soon as possible—and then we can start to untangle this mess." Cummings flipped his pad closed and returned it to his back pocket.

"Thank you, I'm glad to hear that," David said, backing away from his intended destination now that he knew Cummings was on the case. "I think I'll go back to my motel room and get some rest. It's been a rough day, and tomorrow probably won't be a walk in the park either."

"Yeah, you do that. And don't leave town. I'll be in touch." Cummings said, tipping his hat.

David turned and crossed through the living room to the front door. As he walked along the path to the driveway, he noticed two men in dark suits wearing mirrored aviator sunglasses. They were standing amid the parked patrol cars in the predawn light. When they spotted David, they immediately moved toward him in lockstep. He was instantly on high alert as he observed their approach.

"How are you doing, Detective Allerton?" one of them said, stepping forward, his arm outstretched in readiness for a handshake. His face was lean and handsome, sporting a thin, stylish beard and moustache. His thick dark hair was combed loosely, and his eyes were unreadable, lost behind the glasses. "I'm FBI Special Agent Vincent Brooks."

David shook his hand. "Pleased to meet you."

Indicating his colleague, Brooks added, "And this is Supervisory Special Agent Sherman Wells."

Wells nodded, extended his hand to shake David's. His hair was jet black and cut short, framing dusky skin peppered with freckles on his cheeks and along the bridge of his long, straight nose. Unlike his partner, he had a trendy look about him, like a magazine model, an impression enhanced by his chic mirrored shades.

"How are you feeling, Mr. Allerton?" Wells asked with a tone of concern that seemed genuine.

David nodded. "I feel better. My eyes aren't as sensitive to the light as they were earlier." Ironically, at that very moment, he was forced to look down to avoid the sweeping glare of the headlights of a car turning on the driveway nearby.

"You claim that Harold Klein implicated himself and Chief Carville in the diamond heist, and the murder of three of their cohorts?" Wells asked.

"Yeah, Klein gave up everybody. He's busy rolling over like a bowling ball in his dining room even as we speak. Wouldn't you be if you were caught cleaning up the corpse of a dead woman in your kitchen?"

"I guess I would," Wells said, "even with a busted nose and a split-open skull."

David grinned. "I think the dead girl put up quite a fight."

"The dead girl."

"Well, he's a pretty tough guy, you know."

"Yeah, he looks it," Wells replied.

"You see," Agent Brooks said, looking around to see if anyone was in earshot, "Labrec was a close friend of ours. He was the one who referred us to Richard Whitehouse, who consulted on several of our cases. So it's hard to swallow that he was in cahoots with Klein in the commission of such heinous crimes."

David shrugged and sighed. "Then it just goes to show, gentlemen, you should never be too sure about who you trust, even if they're wearing a badge." Flexing his arms and then massaging his right shoulder, he added, "I hope you guys don't mind; but if you don't have any more questions, I'd like to go home and get some sleep."

"Oh sure, no problem." Agent Wells stepped aside to allow David access to the parked cars on the street behind him. "Mainly, we just wanted to meet you and congratulate you on a job well done."

"Thanks."

As David walked off, both men watched him leave. When he was out of range, Wells remarked to Brooks, "He seemed normal to me."

"Yeah, I agree. I think Klein is coming apart. All that shit about Allerton talking to himself and brutally assaulting him is just his way of trying to discredit him."

"Oh, but I think he did beat the shit out of Klein," Wells countered. "It didn't appear to be the work of a woman to me."

"So what? Klein's a shit. He killed an unarmed woman in cold blood. He got less than what he deserved."

"Well, in any case, let's leave it all up to the Rutland PD," Wells said with a note of finality in his voice, as he turned to glance at the front of the house where Klein was being led out in handcuffs, flanked by three officers. They crossed the lawn and headed toward a squad car. Wells added, "They obviously have everything under control here. I'm flying back to Washington."

"Yeah, you do that," Brooks said indifferently. "I might stay to attend the funeral in a few hours. You can think what you want about Richard, but he did a lot of good work for us."

Wells looked thoughtful. "Yeah, you're right about that. You're really planning on going?"

"Yeah, I think I will," Brooks said decisively.

"Maybe I'll postpone leaving for a day or two and go with you," Wells said, as they headed to their vehicle.

THE DEAD WEAR BLACK TUXEDOS

Standing in the bathroom of the motel room, Kevin struggled with his black tie in the mirror. He also toyed with a strand of hair that would not lie down. Meanwhile, in the front room, Margaret stirred in one of the two beds, stretched her legs languidly and sat up slowly. Her long dark hair was disheveled, and her face looked relatively plain without makeup. She glanced around in confusion for a moment at the unfamiliar surroundings. When she spotted David sprawled on the other single bed, she soon realized where she was.

"What time is it?" she shouted in the general direction of the bathroom, yawning.

"Six thirty in the morning," Kevin replied matter-of-factly.

"Six thirty?" she exclaimed, immediately slipping her legs out from under the covers and heading into the bathroom in her heavy cotton nightshirt.

Kevin finally gave up on any further tweaking of his tie or his hair. He shouldered past Margaret impatiently to check himself out in the full-length mirror in the front room, paying special attention to his shiny patent leather shoes and the creases in his slacks. He was anxious, nervous—ready to pounce. Today was already wearing on him, the funeral looming in his mind, making it difficult for him to focus on anything else.

Deciding with a sense of relief that his appearance passed muster, Kevin turned his attention on David, still fast asleep in a tangle of sheets and strewn pillows, his dark, muscular limbs hanging off the edge of the bed. He knew that David had probably only recently climbed into bed and he hated to disturb him. But he had to have his questions answered before he left or they would percolate all day. He kicked at David's foot hanging over the edge of the bed, eliciting a grumble. Kevin did it again, this time eliciting more of a response.

"David," Kevin said, "what happened last night?"

"Sheriff Cummings showed up, cleaned up every-thing..." David groaned as he came awake.

"Are they going to the beach house to look for Carville?"

"I don't know," he mumbled.

Kevin persisted. "What about Harold Klein? Did they file charges?"

"They're going to. First-degree murder—they have the evidence. His registered gun, his house, his crime." David rolled over so his back faced Kevin—an unsubtle hint to back off.

While Kevin was deciding whether to prod him again, he heard a knock on the front door. He gave up on David and went to open it, finding himself face to face with his cousin Paul. For some reason, he looked smaller than usual in his black tuxedo, white frilled shirt, and his very own crooked bow tie.

"Ready?" Paul asked, grinning broadly at the sight of his cousin all dressed up.

Kevin nodded as he reached out to straighten Paul's tie. Then he shut the door behind him and followed his cousin across the lot to where his uncle's car patiently awaited them, its engine running. Since his uncle Nick was behind the wheel and his aunt Charity held down the shotgun position, the two slipped into the backseat next to Linda.

"How did you sleep, Kevin?" Nick asked as he pulled away from the curb. "Your eyes look terrible."

Kevin touched his tender eyelids, grimacing. "Allergies."

"You haven't been crying all night have you?" Linda inquired sympathetically.

"Whatever, Linda," Kevin replied.

"I'm just not ready for this," Nick said, his tone tinged with sadness.

"Neither am I," Kevin readily agreed.

Paul interjected, "Are you coming back to our house after the funeral?"

"I'm working on an investigation right now, buddy, so no," Kevin explained.

"How's that coming along?" Nick asked.

"It's an open investigation, Uncle Nick. I can't talk about it."

"Oh, that's right, I understand."

All voices fell silent after this, which was fine with Kevin, who did not feel like playing thirty questions all the way to the funeral, which is what preoccupied him at the moment. Since there were scant human remains from the explosion, it would be a closed casket service. His uncle seemed eager to minimize the pain by arranging for a priest who was known for performing a fifteen-minute ceremony instead of one lasting two hours. This was good for Kevin in more ways than one, since he felt he could do far more to honor his father's memory by getting on with his investigation than spending lots of time at his graveside.

Soon the car came to a stop amid a collection of other vehicles, and the family filed out. Nick took the lead, accompanied by his wife and daughter, his arms draped over their shoulders as they walked. Kevin and Paul followed behind them into the church. When the family entered, there was a sudden hush as all conversation ceased, and people found their seats as the organ music began to play.

Kevin looked around in amazement at the huge number of mourners in attendance. It was as if the entire town had emptied out to come here and fill every inch of the spacious church. The family went to the front row of pews and sat down together solemnly.

Once settled in his seat, Kevin had a chance to observe his surroundings. The church was old and rustic, and far too warm. A huge ceiling fan whirred overhead but did little to cool the room. There was the not unpleasant smell of earth, as if the church itself was a part of nature.

The mourners sat quietly, heads bowed before the long, shiny black coffin, covered with an American flag. Fresh flowers were arranged all around it, accompanied by cards and notes from people giving their condolences.

Presently, the minister came out, stepping smoothly onto the dais and taking his place behind the lectern. He raised his eyes and hands heavenward and, true to his reputation, gave a stirring, shouting, marching back-and-forth kind of sermon that was so moving and compelling that fifteen minutes passed in no time.

When he was finished, the minister wiped his brow. Several deacons came up front to move the flowers and cards, so the pallbearers could lift the coffin and carry it down the center aisle of the church. The family rose and followed the pallbearers outside. They watched as the coffin was transferred to the hearse, which soon pulled away.

Nick shook hands and received many affectionate pats on the back from members of the solicitous crowd who were congregating at the entrance to the church. Charity and Linda exchanged loving hugs with some, while others fondly ruffled Paul's neatly combed hair. Only a very few people stopped to tell the stoical, red-eyed Kevin Whitehouse they were sorry for his loss.

In the distance, across the road, were the two FBI agents, Wells and Brooks, simply staring.

"I can't believe what I'm seeing," Brooks said.

"They're calling him Kevin Whitehouse, not David Allerton."

"Maybe he's part of the family?" Brooks frowned and looked perplexed. He thought, but didn't say, that David Allerton looked exactly like Kevin Whitehouse; that he was no doubt playing some kind of game posing as two people— probably to fool the police.

"Today," Wells sneered, "he's Kevin Whitehouse, son of Richard. And yet last night he was masquerading as David Allerton, New York City detective."

"You mean, private investigator, now deputy," Brooks clarified.

"Whatever... the fact is he's masquerading as two

people," Wells said, visibly angry at the idea that he must be getting away with something and yet they couldn't unmask him.

"The question is, why?"

Wells shook his head in exasperation. "Listen, I've got to go..."

Wells started moving forward, but Brooks placed a restraining hand at his elbow that made him pause. "No, you don't."

He turned on Brooks. "This is some kind of scam, Vincent. This guy is playing some kind of jurisdictional ballgame here where he's the umpire!"

"And what?" Brooks challenged. "You want to throw away your advantage by charging into his little game and breaking it up before the last inning? This guy seems to be hot balls on top of retrieving those diamonds, and maybe he's doing it for himself. But he may be the only chance we'll ever get to recover them."

"So you think he's a rogue part of their team?" Wells asked.

"Quite possibly playing the law, just like Carville."

Both men fell silent momentarily as they pondered that thought.

Then Brooks shook his head. "I still can't believe this shit about Labrec."

"Yeah, I could have sworn that he was a straight shooter too." Wells reached into his jacket and pulled out his mirrored sunshades. Slipping them on, he turned his chiseled features again in Kevin's direction. "But if he's dirty, we've got to expose him."

"Let's go do some homework, starting with his superiors in New York City," Brooks said, "That's *if* he has any superiors there."

Meanwhile, Kevin wandered over to his uncle's car and leaned against it. When he felt he was free from prying eyes, he turned his back on the throng of people still milling about outside the church, and retrieved his cell phone to call David.

"Who the fuck is this?" David growled, annoyed at being awakened again.

"It's me," Kevin replied.

"I thought you were at the funeral. Why are you calling me now?"

"I forgot to ask you before if Klein implicated Carville."

David sighed tiredly. "When they took Harold to the jail, word on the street was that he sang like a canary."

"Do you think we can get the transcript of his interview?"

"Shit if I know. Why don't you drop by and see?"

"Good idea, maybe I will," said Kevin.

"How was the funeral?"

"Nobody fainted in the presence of the holy spirit, if that's what you want to know."

David chuckled. "I'll see you in a few hours. Where do you think you'll be?"

"Back at the motel room."

"I'll meet you here then."

David hung up just seconds before Nick approached Kevin and started patting him gently on the shoulder. "Ready to leave?" he asked.

"Yeah, I'm tired."

"You really look like shit around the eyes."

"Allergies, like I said."

They slipped into the car and waited for the others to join them.

Nick looked up into the rearview mirror, adjusting it so that he could see Kevin clearly. "You know my brother didn't kill himself, don't you?"

"That much I do know, Uncle."

"He would never have done such a thing."

"I know."

The two fell silent after that.

"They've issued a BOLO for Carville. He didn't report to work, and if that isn't incriminating, nothing is," David said. He was sitting behind the wheel of their rental car, driving at dusk along the poorly lit country roads. It was late evening on the day of the funeral.

Kevin, seated beside him, nodded his understanding. "But is anyone watching Hepner's beach house right now in case he's there searching for the diamonds?"

David shrugged his shoulders. "I don't know."

"So, why are *we* going up there?" Margaret asked from the backseat.

"To join in the search—duh. And to make sure we're there in case nobody else is," David said.

Margaret shook her head ruefully at David's flippancy and sat back with a huff, gazing out her side window.

"We have a total of six people involved—right, David?" Kevin asked.

"Yeah, I think so. We have your father, Willie Hamilton,

Trip Hepner, Katherine Werthers, Harold Klein, and Sheriff Carville," David enumerated.

"I've got a question," Kevin said. "When do you think Klein and Carville discovered the diamonds were in jeopardy?"

"Obviously, it had to be recently, since that's when all the bodies started turning up."

Kevin mulled that over. "Katherine Werthers and Willie Hamilton got together, and they went to Glitter-Gun. So I wonder why my father was the first to be killed. It doesn't make sense."

"Maybe your father's role ran deeper than you think. Maybe he and Glitter-Gun were the ones hiding part or all of the diamonds," David suggested; "and in addition to stone-walling Willie about the location of the gems, your father threatened to tell Hepner that Willie was after a premature withdrawal. That gives Hamilton an even stronger motive for murder."

Kevin chuckled bitterly. "So shit-for-brains, third-grade graduate Willie Hamilton rigs my father's garage to explode with him in it?"

"Wait, I have another idea," David said. "Maybe there's another player—someone completely unknown to us right now."

"A seventh person?" Kevin replied, obviously puzzled at the idea.

"Yeah. Someone who was watching over them all."

"Well, I agree we *are* missing something crucial here."

"Well, here we are." David turned into the driveway toward a cordon of police cars. As he pulled up, he was flagged down by two uniformed officers, one of whom approached him and asked for his identification. As he handed over his Brandon PD identification, the other officer walked along the passenger side of the vehicle and shined his flashlight across Kevin and then Margaret, who sat perfectly still in the back. He continued to sweep the beam of light around the rest of the interior, including the floor, actively searching for something. Presently, he looked over the top of the vehicle and nodded to his partner, who was finishing up with David.

Once he got his ID back, David pulled away to find a parking space.

"You can breathe now, Margaret," Kevin said.

"I just don't like it when they shine the light in my face," she said, sounding uncharacteristically subdued.

As David parked their vehicle, he said to Kevin, "Get me the Glock from the glove compartment."

Kevin popped open the glove compartment and handed the pistol over to David.

"What's the plan?" Margaret asked.

"Look around for clues, or for any place where six million in glass can be hidden," David said, pulling back the action on the Glock and checking for a bullet in the chamber. Once satisfied it was there, he added, "Let's go."

They headed up the rise of sandy soil and beach grass to an imposing house on the shore supported by pylons at least seven feet high. The two-story structure featured two balconies, the lower one a raised, roofless porch jutting out over the nearby lake. They soon encountered a flight of stairs that led to it and the front door. They climbed slowly and quietly in the dark, and when they reached the door, they found it unlocked. David entered first, followed by Kevin and Margaret.

The three found themselves in a spacious room where three Rutland officers were clearly in the middle of a search, which came to an abrupt halt when they spotted the newcomers. David, again showing his ID, explained their mission to the one who approached them. He waved them on and resumed his activities as the trio went off in different directions to pursue their own agendas.

After an hour on the premises, Kevin announced his intention to go out and get something to drink; so he asked around to see if anyone else wanted anything. The officers from Rutland grunted in the negative, Margaret politely declined, but David requested a beer. Kevin left the house and stood on the elevated porch for a moment, staring up at the bright slice of moon in an otherwise cloudless sky. He thought about where the nearest Kwik-Stop might be, figuring it couldn't be too far off. As he took the stairs one cautious step at a time, he heard an unexpected sound in the distance, the unmistakable sound of someone digging.

Fortunately, the moon lit up the night with a silvery hue, but he needed something that could focus light on his immediate surroundings as he scanned for the sound through the darkness underneath the house. Then he remembered the penlight on his keychain and reached into his pants pocket to retrieve it. He rounded the stair and moved stealthily forward, keeping it pointed downward and away from him as he proceeded.

Up ahead, under the house, the digging grew louder, and Kevin slowly made his way toward it. He crouched lower, and synchronized his steps with the rasping noise of the shovel as it scraped the sand.

Then he heard a voice call, "Who's there?"—and the shoveling stopped.

Kevin stood upright to reveal himself, holding up his penlight and aiming it in the direction of the man's voice. A youthful officer burst into view in the small circle of light, a spade shovel in hand and appearing quite nervous.

"Wha... what... who are you?" he stammered, wielding the shovel like a weapon.

"Never mind who I am. Who are *you*?"

"Officer Peter Weeks, Rutland PD... now it's your turn."

"I'm Kevin Whitehouse, a Brandon PD deputy," he said as he swept the area of the sand where Weeks was digging with the beam of light. "So what are you doing out here? Did you find some sort of clue that sent you digging in this spot?"

The officer remained silent.

"What's the matter? Why don't you answer me?" Kevin persisted.

Kevin froze as he felt something hard pressed against the back of his head. Very slowly, he turned his head to peer over his shoulder, where he saw Labrec Carville behind him, a stubby Smith & Wesson SD40 VE in his hand. He was dressed in a khaki-colored coverall, evidently prepped for the work at hand.

"Too smart for your own good, eh, *High-Powered*? Get your hands up where I can see them."

"Maybe so," Kevin admitted.

"Drop your flashlight on the ground."

Kevin obeyed, saying, "Don't you know this area is crawling with personnel from Rutland PD? How could you think you could dig around here and not get caught?"

"Shut up and turn around!" Carville snarled, shifting his weight from one foot to the other, and opening and closing his grip on the gnarly handgun.

Kevin faced him woodenly, and as he did he suddenly noticed with surprise the butt end of the Glock protruding from his own belt. How in the hell did that get there? he wondered. Did David plant it on him before he left the house?

Now the tension out there in the dark was thick as fog.

"Okay," Carville said calmly, "using only your pinky finger, remove the Glock."

With very little difficulty Kevin pulled the gun from behind his belt and let it fall to the sand at his feet.

"Now kick it over here."

Kevin kicked the gun, which didn't travel far in the sand. "Who's helping you, Labrec, besides Weeks over here?"

"Help? I don't need help."

"Who's the other guy?" Kevin pressed.

"What other guy?"

"The seventh man—the one who's in on the heist with you. Or is it this guy here?" Kevin asked, pointing at Weeks, although he looked like an unlikely candidate.

"I'm not helping anyone," Weeks replied nervously, his eyes darting back and forth between the two men. "I was checking out under the house and this guy gets the drop on me."

"Shaddup, and don't you worry about that, *High-Powered*," Carville advised him.

Carville stooped low to pick up the Glock and the penlight, and then backed away. "This is good. This is very good." After pocketing the two items, he walked over to a pile of shovels, picked one up and tossed it so it landed at Kevin's feet. "Hey, *High-Powered!* Get to work!"

Kevin looked around in the dark, but there was no one else in sight. It was evident that the Rutland PD had focused their search on the inside of the house, while the two officers outside were closer to the road and very far from where Kevin stood. He reached down and took stock of the distance between himself and Carville, who he noticed had made a point of keeping a position just clear of the swing of the shovel should Kevin become so daring.

Noticing Kevin's inaction, Carville hissed, "Get to digging!" He waved the gun, steering Kevin toward Weeks, who was digging close to a pylon.

Kevin took up a position just on the other side of him, driving the spade shovel into the earth. He kicked it down with his heel, pushing it deeper, and then pried the sand up, tossing it aside.

"Okay, Carville… why kill my father and Willie Hamilton?"

"Keep digging, I said."

"But why kill them?" Kevin asked again.

"I didn't kill them. I didn't kill *anybody*. Do you understand me?"

"So you don't know who the seventh person is, do you?"

"There is no seventh person!" Carville sighed in exasperation. "Now stop with the fucking talking! You're here to work."

"Why, Carville? What are you going to do to me if I don't dig? Shoot me?" Kevin challenged.

"Yeah."

"With all these cops around here? How far do you think you'll get?"

Another voice spoke up off to the right and a little behind Carville: "You wouldn't get far, Labrec, trust me."

Carville turned his head in the direction of the speaker; and although the body was lost in the shadows under the house, he could see the weak light of the moon upon the oily black surface of a Chiappa M9-22 semi-auto pistol with a sound suppressor elongating the muzzle.

"Drop the gun, Labrec," the voice whispered.

"And what if I don't?" Carville's gun was still trained on Kevin.

"Don't make me shoot you just because you think you can frighten me. Trust me, no one will hear my bullets tear open your chest. Now drop the gun."

Carville dropped the Smith & Wesson.

"And the Glock."

The Glock and the penlight followed the Smith & Wesson to the sand.

"Take a step back." The lengthy muzzle waved Carville away.

He backed up and the gunman came forward, joining the clique of men under the house.

Kevin registered the gunman with a shock of recognition as he emerged from the shadows. It was his father, Richard, who stepped into the puddle of penlight that now illuminated them all.

CORPUS DELICTI

"Dad?" Kevin gasped.

Richard gazed at his son and smiled. "Good to see you, son."

"Cigarette Burns?" Carville exclaimed.

Kevin stood dumbstruck as he took in his father. He looked older, of course, and yet somehow better than his son remembered. His clean-shaven face sported a mischievous smile, and his eyes fairly sparkled at seeing Kevin.

"Dad, I thought you were dead," was all Kevin could manage.

"Not right now I'm not." Richard quickly retrieved the weapons and the penlight from the ground—one at a time— and stashed the guns in his pockets. He held the penlight in his left hand. "You two are going to work now," he said, indicating Carville and Weeks.

"You mean, you know where the diamonds are?" Carville asked in genuine surprise.

"I'm thinking pylons too," Richard responded. "Now pick up one of those fucking shovels, Carville."

The chief looked glumly at his captor and bent down for one of the shovels.

"Dad, how in the world did you get mixed up in all of this?" Kevin asked in disbelief.

Richard sighed, ignored the question. "Kevin, go over there and pick up one of those shovels."

Kevin looked at his father for a moment, trying to read the man, then walked over and snatched a shovel from the sand.

Richard waved his gun muzzle around. "Alright, now stand together and head in that direction." He motioned with his gun toward an area further under the pylons. The two men trudged off in the indicated direction, with Kevin and his father following close behind.

"You killed Willie?" Carville asked Richard over his shoulder.

"Prick tried to kill me. He had every intention of taking all of the diamonds for himself," Richard said.

"Then why fake your death, Dad?" Kevin asked.

"Because of Klein and Carville, who set up Trip from the beginning," he explained hotly. "The Liberians were looking to launder their diamonds here. Six million in dirty diamonds—so-called blood diamonds—in exchange for five million in clean American currency. It was easy. The Liberians would give their diamonds to the Franklin Bank, have someone steal them who would hand them back to them, and they could then collect the insurance and pay off the robbers. But Klein and Carville, those fucks, never intended to make good on the deal. Instead, they came up with a plan to rip off the Liberians themselves.

"Next, they had to get Glitter-Gun to make up the crew.

So Klein tells Trip about the diamonds, and where it's going to happen, that all Trip needs to do is to find a few gullible idiots to do the job and they'll all walk away with six million in diamonds. But what Trip didn't know is that Carville and Klein were in it for themselves."

"One problem," Carville interjected. "What was in it for us?"

"Everything," Richard continued. "You must have given Trip some stupid-assed percentage, that we'd all split the money, but it was your intention to rip him and his crew off within the five years."

"That's true?" Kevin asked Carville, who looked down and didn't answer.

"That's right, son. They were going to wait a while and when the time was right, steal the diamonds from Trip and the Liberians. What would the rest of us do? Confess to the authorities that we robbed the diamonds from the Franklin vault and then were ripped off ourselves? That's tantamount to a confession. And when word got out that their loot was stolen, the Liberians would've hunted us down in the streets or in the jails—or wherever we tried to hide—in retaliation.

"This crafty fuck"— Richard jabbed the back of Carville's head with the muzzle of his gun to goad him—"goes to Katherine and offers her a million dollars on top of her existing cut to get hard-up Willie Hamilton to speed up the timeline. Money he never intended to give her. The plan was that she and Willie would approach Trip, who would feel warm-hearted toward the loving couple, and readily indulge their request that he hand over their share of the diamonds immediately—thereby disclosing their location for Klein and Carville to grab them. But Willie got greedy and dangerous before you could, right, Carville? He killed Trip while he was trying to find out where the diamonds were hidden, and there went the only man who knew where the fuck they were."

"How do you fit into all this, Dad?" Kevin asked, reluctant to hear his reply.

"One July Fourth, I overheard Carville and Klein talking during a fireworks display. They didn't know I was nearby and could hear them. They spoke freely about how they were going to move in on the diamonds in another two years, and make sure that we'd be the ones who'd take the rap for the heist. I thought, fuck that, and gave myself a new identity."

As they reached one of the pylons, Richard broke off his narrative abruptly and ordered his captives to stop. The two men halted in their tracks, their shovels at the ready. He beamed the penlight up and down the pylon until he found the spot where a 3 was stenciled on it.

"Start digging," he ordered.

"Why here?" Carville asked.

"Stop asking questions—just start digging," Richard replied impatiently.

Carville and Weeks drove the points of their shovels into the sand. Kevin had held on to his shovel and decided he might as well pitch in, propelled by curiosity if nothing else. Maybe his father really did know where the diamonds were buried. So he dug on the other side of the pylon, bringing up damp sand rapidly.

"Why stage your own death, Dad?" Kevin tried this question again as he tossed another load off to the side.

"Shit, son, Carville is the *police chief*. Do you think if the plan started to unravel he would have any compunction about killing us off and burying our bodies in some remote part of Brandon Town Forest? Add to it that the Liberians are not the most congenial people, and what can really piss them off are smart-assed white people trying to rip off their diamonds. Either you disappear or die—like I did—before anyone can find you.

"When Willie Hamilton was suspected of breaking into the bank three years ago, this motherfucker," indicating Carville, "started out manipulating and misplacing evidence to get him acquitted. Because how smart would it be to have the cops sniffing around old Trip the jeweler—Willie's old pal—with six million dollars of diamonds up his ass. Nope, he faded the heat, and Willie Hamilton never found out who, why, or what helped him stay out of jail. He was the consummate fall guy.

"I figured I would be fingered as the explosives expert in this joyride as soon as Carville and Klein made their escape—so I had to vanish, and vanish without a trace. I began frequenting the seedier parts of Brandon until one night I met a homeless guy of approximately my build, age and race, and I coaxed him back to my house for a hot shower, a decent meal, and a comfortable bed."

Kevin grimaced in horror. "So you lured him into your house to masquerade as your dead body?"

Richard turned to Weeks, and started waving his gun at him angrily. "Dig deeper, faster!"

The officer redoubled his efforts.

"So what are we going to do out here all night, Cigarette?" Carville groused. "Dig our own graves too?"

"Yeah, why not? You surely would have planted me in one if you were given half the chance," Richard quipped.

"So, Dad, it was the homeless guy who was blown up in your garage?" Kevin couldn't seem to stop himself from asking more unpleasant questions, as if he hoped at some point he'd get an answer he could live with.

"Yes, son, the body was his. I had wired the garage several days before, so I'd have time to get everything ready. After a good night's sleep, I cooked the guy a hearty breakfast and then plied him with Scotch—his drink of choice—until he was falling down drunk. I took him to the garage, sat him down at the workbench half-conscious, stuffed my wallet into his back pocket, put my hat on his head, my watch around his wrist, set the timer and the rest was history. From then on, I stayed up in Brandon Town Forest in a little shack I'd built to hide out in years ago in case of a nuclear holocaust."

Listening carefully to his words and beginning to grasp his worldview, Kevin began to think his father might be seriously mentally ill. Somewhere along the line he had slipped up and his thinking had become demented. That had to be the only explanation.

"So, after you get up one morning and kill an innocent man, you follow it up with murdering Willie?" Carville remarked, shaking his head in distaste.

"No! I didn't set out to hurt Willie. I just wanted to talk to him, but he's a hardheaded motherfucker. It was after he'd seen Glitter-Gun, thinking like the guy had the diamonds in his dresser drawer or his front pocket. When Hepner didn't come up with them, Willie killed him. Can you believe that? Glitter-Gun never hurt anyone." Richard sounded truly dismayed, as if he cared about his friend, after all, and as if his was the only death in the whole scenario that really mattered.

"So I went to this prick's trailer, hoping he'd still be there and hadn't yet gone off to get the diamonds—*if* he knew where they were. He was still there, seeming reasonable at first; but he must have sensed I was there to stop him from getting the loot because the fuck tried to brain me with a beer bottle; and when that didn't work, he tried to gas me to death inside his home."

"So what's your plan, Cigarette?" Carville asked fearlessly, resting his body momentarily against the handle of his shovel. "If you get the diamonds, what are you going to do, kill us and disappear?"

"No, just disappear."

Kevin piped up with another question. "How'd you get the name Cigarette Burns, Dad?"

"His fingers are all yellow from smoking," Carville explained matter-of-factly. "That was his nickname since after high school."

"Stop digging!" Richard said disgustedly. "This isn't working out."

"This isn't working out for any of us," Carville agreed. "You've got blood on your hands, Cigarette. Why don't you just turn yourself in?"

"*You* are complicit in at least one murder, Labrec!" Richard countered. "You're not playing good cop here tonight, buddy. If I get caught, I'm nailing your ass to the wall."

"You're a felon, Cigarette Burns. Your word doesn't mean shit in court."

As the two men argued, Kevin saw motion from the

corner of his eye, a figure in the shadows, ducking from one pylon to another. He turned his head almost imperceptibly to get a better look and saw that it was David stealthily approaching the group.

The embittered exchange between Carville and his father became just background noise as Kevin focused surreptitiously on David, who was signaling to him with his hands. Kevin frowned when it appeared that David wanted him to plow into his father.

Suddenly, both Carville and Richard noticed Kevin's facial expressions and darting eyes. They followed his gaze toward where David was hiding, trying to catch a glimpse of whatever it was Kevin was seeing there. But they saw nothing but shadows.

It was then that Kevin launched himself at his father, the side of his hand chopping down on the wrist holding the gun, his shoulder plowing into his father's chest, sending them both sprawling on the sand.

The gun seemed to fly out of Richard's hand and disappear into the darkness. But Carville and Weeks, intent on its trajectory, spotted where it landed and made a mad dash for it.

David darted out from behind a pylon as Carville, now on his knees with officer Weeks, head-butted him, breaking the bridge of the officer's nose. If anyone thought he was Carville's confederate, they knew better now.

As officer Weeks fell away, Carville surged to his feet with the Chiappa M9-22 in hand. He whipped around, training the gun on Kevin and Richard just as David tackled him from behind. He struck him low at the thighs with his shoulder, lifting him off his feet and flipping him over on his back to crash prone on the ground—but still holding the gun. The wind knocked out of him, Carville rolled over, dazed and battered from the fall. David seized the opportunity to step down hard on his gun hand, crushing it and grinding it with the toe of his shoe. Carville cried out in pain and released the Chiappa, cradling his injured hand.

"For fuck's sake!" David called to Weeks as he dropped to his knees, landing on Carville's solar plexus. "Get your ass up and give me your handcuffs!"

Weeks, wiping blood away from his broken nose, rose to his feet and staggered over to David. He helped him cuff the chief's hands behind his back.

David snatched up the Chiappa and called out to Kevin, who was standing nearby, looking around in the dark for his father. But Richard was nowhere in sight.

"Did you see where your father went, Kevin?" David asked in an urgent tone.

"No, I don't know," Kevin said as looked around frantically, finally stopping to gaze steadily at the shoreline, which seemed the most likely escape route. "Maybe he headed over there."

Kevin suddenly remembered his penlight, and where it had fallen in the sand. He went over and picked it up before charging off toward the water with David right behind him. Soon they were out from under the house, on the open stretch of sand that led down to the lake.

"Do you think he came by boat?" Kevin gasped for air as he ran.

"I would have," David replied, not the least bit winded.

As they reached the shore, Kevin shone the light down the coastline to the left, finding nothing in close range.

"Are you certain he went this way?" David asked.

"I think he *might* have run off in this direction, but I'm not sure. It's just that I don't see how he could've gone anywhere else without being seen or getting caught." Kevin beamed the light on the other side, and some distance away, behind a fallen tree trunk, he thought he saw movement. "David," he whispered, "do you see something over there?"

Nodding, David bolted off with Kevin right beside him. They saw a head emerge from behind the log and then drop from sight. As they closed the distance between themselves and their quarry, they heard the rattle and roar of an outboard. Accompanied by a rugged hum, a Saturn inflatable motorboat in the shape of a bloated letter A shot from behind the log, driven by its outboard towards the silvery black center of the lake.

David leaped over the log, aiming in a two-handed grip at the departing boat, and getting off several shots. Fireballs came toward him—Richard blasting back—splinters of wood bursting from the log behind him. Kevin, fearlessly braving the bullets zipping around him, came up alongside David and struck down the muzzle of his gun, which drilled the earth at his feet twice.

"What the fuck are you doing, Kevin?" David snarled.

"That's my father you're shooting at!"

"He's a murderer and a felon. He needs to be stopped!"

"But not this way, David, not this way."

David sighed, turning to watch the outboard keep to the far side of the lake as it moved through the water at full throttle before disappearing from view. He turned to head back to the beach house, looking dejected. "Maybe we can get the Coast Guard on his ass."

As Kevin fell into step beside him, he said accusingly, "You'd shoot my father, wouldn't you?"

"He had a gun on people—that means he's a threat."

"But you started shooting first."

"Oh, what a poor unfortunate turn of events for him. Maybe next time."

"David, sometimes I think you have a total disregard for human life."

"Yep, buddy, that's right. Everyone's but my own. Everyone's but my own."

The rest of the Rutland police department had descended upon the beach house like falling rain. Carville was led from the house in handcuffs once there were enough cars for a police escort. He moved woodenly through a throng of reporters from the neighboring towns. He turned away as they pounded him with questions and camera flashes, until he was able to duck into the backseat of the squad car designated for him, grateful when the door closed solidly after him.

Darryl Bates, Brandon's only roving news reporter, was allotted a room in the beach house that served as his field of operations for interviews and information-gathering. Mayor Michael Gillette was seen leaving the room, wringing his hands and wiping sweat from his forehead after being hammered with questions regarding his police chief and that other pillar of the law, Harold Klein.

When he caught a glimpse of Peter Weeks in the hallway outside his room, Darryl rose quickly and caught the officer by the elbow before he could get away. Weeks turned toward him with deep purple eye sockets and a bandaged nose, his nostrils stuffed with cotton.

"Please, please, can I get just a minute of your time?" Bates pleaded.

"I don't know," Weeks replied weakly, in no mood to talk with anyone.

Bates knew that he had him. "You've got a story to tell, Officer Weeks. We just want to hear it."

Weeks looked about wearily, as if for some last-minute reprieve, before entering the room resignedly. "Okay. What do you want to know?"

Bates guided the officer to a mark on the floor in front of the TV camera, ran his fingers back through his hair, and stuck the microphone into Weeks' face.

"What happened in those desperate moments under the beach house, Officer Weeks?"

"It was hard to tell... everything moved too fast. Richard Whitehouse"—he looked around for someone to correct him—"had the gun on the three of us and then everything spun out of control."

"How?"

"The deputy, Kevin Whitehouse, was a whirling dervish. He seemed to be everywhere at once, and then he was off, chasing his father down to the shoreline."

"Do you think because he was chasing his father that he let him get away?"

"I can't answer that."

"I understand."

"I really have to leave now—thank you." Weeks waved at the camera feebly, turned, and left the room.

Bates followed him out onto the balcony and watched as Kevin was escorted outside by a knot of police officers. He returned to the room quickly and told the cameraman to get his camera outside pronto. Waving him on, he slipped out after him, pushing through the crowd of onlookers until he was right up in Kevin's face, holding the microphone under his chin.

"Is it true, Mr. Whitehouse, that you let your father slip through your fingers?"

"No comment," Kevin replied calmly as he kept walking, despite being jostled about by the mob.

"Where was your partner David Allerton during this time?"

Kevin ignored the question as he was ushered into a waiting squad car, thankful when it pulled away from the driveway of the beach house.

"Did they ever find the diamonds?" Kevin asked the officers in the front seat.

"Not yet. Everyone's still looking," the officer on the passenger side replied, adding, "and trust me, they won't stop until they find them."

Kevin grew thoughtful as he sat there, reflecting on what had just transpired and David's decision that it would be prudent for Kevin to take the heat on this one. Since his father was involved, people would likely be sympathetic toward his behavior. Before they parted, David had turned over the Chiappa to him and headed rapidly down the shoreline, finally vanishing into the moonlit dark.

Several officers met up with Kevin as he approached the house solo. They were hopped up on adrenaline, their mouths running like the outboard behind his father's skiff.

Kevin, feeling numb at this point, fell silent as they led him up the stairs to a bedroom inside the house, where they disarmed him and a doctor checked him over for injuries. Then he gave a preliminary statement before Mayor Gillette dropped by to shake his hand. Once they were done, he was escorted down to the squad car where he now found himself.

In time, which felt almost like an eternity, he was brought to the Brandon police department. He was led to a room with a table and chair, where he was invited to sit. There was another chair against one wall, and across from it a mirrored wall—clearly a one-way mirror with an unknown number of observers on the other side.

Shortly, the door opened and Kevin was relieved to see a familiar face in the threshold. It was his old friend, Captain Sam Jefferies. Kevin figured his untidy appearance meant he'd come up to Vermont in a hurry, not having time enough to comb his curly salt and pepper hair, which stuck out at odd angles from his head. His cheeks were unshaven, and his eyes were tired and looked more sunken than usual. He smiled broadly at Kevin as he slipped inside the room, unbuttoning his jacket at the stomach, and taking a seat in the only other available chair.

"Kevin," he said cautiously, "it's good to see you."

"Yes, Sam, you too."

"I've brought a friend with me."

"Who—Margaret?" Kevin ventured.

At that moment, the stocky diminutive figure of Dr. Fagen stepped into the room. He smiled warmly at Kevin, who noticed that his brownish-red beard seemed to get whiter each time they met.

"Hello, Kevin," Fagen said jovially.

"Oh, no, Doc. No more mind games, please," Kevin said before turning to Jefferies to add, "When do I get debriefed and out of here?"

"Immediately—as soon as you tell us what happened under the house and at the lakefront," Jefferies said.

"Under the house... everything happened so fast, I just stepped away and it was over."

"This contradicts Officer Weeks, who says you single-handedly disarmed two men."

"I don't remember that."

"I think I know why, Kevin," Jefferies said. "It's because you weren't there alone."

Kevin smiled. "You know it, Sam. He was there."

Dr. Fagen spoke up first. "You mean David?"

"Who else would I be talking about, Doc?"

"Just checking."

"Okay, Kevin. So what did David do?" Jefferies began anew with a voice of soft authority.

"Well, after he disarmed the men, he and I chased my father to the edge of the lake where he had a boat moored. My father hopped in and tore out of there, and David tried to shoot either him or the boat, but he got away."

"Did you know that David is waiting just outside?" Dr. Fagen said.

"He is?" Kevin's face lit up. "He can explain more about this than I can. I'm still processing my father being a criminal. I may even be charged as an accessory because of him."

Jefferies shook his head. "Not a chance of that happening. You were working by special request—"

"—special request of Chief Carville!" Kevin finished for him.

"Well, don't forget, Kevin. I was the one who approved the deputizing. That would mean I colluded with the chief, which we know is impossible."

"Kevin," Dr. Fagen interjected, leaning forward, "would you please bring David in for us? We need to debrief him too before he can go."

"Yeah, I'll get him." Kevin, feeling exhausted, rested his hands on his knees and drove his body forward to rise from the chair.

Fagen and Jefferies watched Kevin round the table, cross the room, and open the door. He stood there momentarily as if he had forgotten something, then closed the door. When he turned around to the two men, he seemed transformed. He held himself straighter and with more confidence—his head held high, his shoulders squared, his chin tilted upward in an attitude of defiance. He strode back to his chair with a swagger that had been absent before. As he seated himself, he said, "Hello, Doc" to Fagen, as if seeing him for the first time.

"Hello, David. It's nice to see you again," Fagen said, as he leaned against the wall and crossed his arms on his chest.

"Didn't I run you out of my apartment last time I saw you?"

"Yes, you did, but I didn't take it personally," Fagen said with a chuckle.

"Well, honestly, you should have." David smirked and turned to Jefferies, who hadn't moved from his chair. "Debriefing time, boss?"

"Yes," Jefferies said.

"What's to tell?" David began. "Old reliable was supposed to go out and get us snacks or something and it was taking him too long. So I went out and found the car still in the driveway. I came back to the house to look around for him outside and find him with his father, who had a gun trained on Carville and another guy.

"I made sure nobody saw me as I moved closer, so that only Kevin could see me." David chuckled, before he continued. "So there I am standing in the dark, motioning with my hands for him to jump his father. Instead of doing it—duh!— Kevin must have made some kind of stupid-assed face, because his father and Carville suddenly look in my direction. That was my cue to take them down. Once I revealed myself—providing a distraction—Kevin knocked the gun out of his father's hand, while I tackled the dipshit sheriff. The next thing I know when I turn around, Richard Whitehouse is gone."

"Which is when you chased him down," Jeffries suggested.

David shrugged. "That's when we ate his dust, to be more exact. By the time I got close enough to get a bead on him in the dark, he was chugging away in a motorboat popping shots back at me. I fired off some of my own, but that was like pulling on a slot machine in Vegas."

"Do you think he got the diamonds?" Jefferies asked.

"Nope. He had everyone digging like there was no tomorrow and they turned up nothing. Besides, no one said that the diamonds were *buried*. For all we know the diamonds might not even be near the house. Trip might have told Willie anything to keep him from killing him—which he eventually did anyway."

"Could be," Jeffries agreed.

David sighed, running a hand over his face. "When do we get out of here, Sam?"

"Soon," Sam replied, crossing his legs. "First, we need you to do us a favor."

"What's that?"

There was a significant pause until Dr. Fagen ventured, "Where is Margaret?"

David looked perplexed. "What are you talking about?"

"Who is she?"

"She's Kevin's squeeze."

"Do you have a... *squeeze*?" Fagen asked.

"There's someone I see from time to time, but she's a snow bunny."

"She's a *snow bunny*?" Jefferies echoed, as if he didn't hear him right.

"Yeah."

"How do you keep her in the flake, David?"

"I have my ways."

Jefferies shook his head. "I didn't hear that."

David laughed.

"Can you describe Margaret for me, David?" Fagen asked.

"She's a skinny, homely looking white girl, with a bad attitude. She doesn't like me and I don't like her back."

"That's an interesting description."

"Fagen wants you to go and bring her here," Jefferies said flatly.

"Me?" David laughed.

"Kevin will refuse us in an effort to protect her," Fagen explained.

David looked at Fagen. "Of course he would, he's her little puppy dog. For all I care, she can just disappear."

Fagen peered at him quizzically. "Why? Would you want that?"

"Yeah, actually I would. She's no good for Kevin."

"Well, regardless of your feelings on the matter, we'd like to get to know her a little bit, if at all possible. When can we see her?" Fagen asked.

David scrunched up his face, narrowed his eyes, and his broad shoulders suddenly went slack. "Why do you want to know? Do you want to make me disappear?"

Both Fagen and Jefferies looked uncomfortable as they heard the softer, more feminine tone of Kevin's voice.

"Are you Margaret?" Fagen asked carefully.

"Yes. And I heard what you said. You want to get rid of me," she replied. Her eyes opened wide, her features softened, she licked her dry lips.

"No, I think you misunderstood me, Margaret," Fagen said carefully. "I said we'd like to get to know you a bit."

"For what reason?" Margaret challenged.

"Well, we know all of Kevin's friends, but you seem to be the most mysterious one."

"Kevin has told me about you, Dr. Fagen," and then turning to Jefferies, "and you too, Sam."

Jefferies smiled.

"Margaret, what is your last name?" Fagen asked.

"Alexander—Margaret Alexander."

"Are you in love with Kevin Whitehouse?"

"Very much so."

"And David?"

"David and I have no special feelings for each other. In fact, I have no feelings for him at all. As far as I'm concerned, he can leave at any time. But you know about the two of them, they're inseparable."

"That's right, but do you know *why* they are that way?" Fagan inquired.

Margaret shook her head.

"Because the two of them are actually one person."

She stared at Fagen, marshaling her thoughts.

"It's true, Margaret. Kevin suffers from Dissociative Identity Disorder, and he has also created you within his psyche, for some reason."

"Dr. Fagen, you realize that David doesn't care very much for you," she said, abruptly changing the subject.

"I don't think that's a correct assessment of my relationship with David. He has some animosity towards me, but it's not that severe."

But Margaret persisted. "He feels that way toward you, Dr. Fagen, because you spend too much time lying to us, twisting things around and talking this psychological mumbo-jumbo just to confuse us."

"Why do you say *us*, Margaret? Shouldn't you say instead, you, Kevin or David?"

"Like I said, you're trying to confuse us," she said, putting the emphasis on *us*. "You're up to something, but we just can't put our finger on it yet."

"Again, Margaret, you keep saying *us* or *we*."

"I'm done, Dr. Fagen," she stated calmly, and then turned

to Jefferies. "Sam, I'm not going to deal with this anymore. I won't talk to Fagen again, I'm not leaving Kevin—and there is nothing you can do about it. Furthermore," she added, as her cold stare moved like ice from Jefferies back to Fagen, "if you do try to *make* me go away, I'll have David do what he does best—kill you both."

The entire room on the other side of the two-way mirror went dead silent after the men witnessed the interview. They were literally mesmerized by the power, grace and sheer otherworldliness of Kevin Whitehouse. They watched in mute surprise as he transitioned from personality to personality—as different from David Allerton as he was from Margaret Alexander. They were clearly three unique and separate personalities, unaware that they existed in the same body, interacting and dealing with each other in their own individual, compartmentalized world. The men in the viewing room were both awed and confused by the individual who had uncovered a diamond heist and a band of murderers, including a man who had faked his own death.

This stunning disposition impelled the men to arrange for a meeting immediately at the mayor's mansion. They drove there in a caravan of SUVs, a short distance from the Brandon police station. The imposing residence was spacious and sprawling, with cream stucco walls and a terra cotta-tiled roof, set amid an abundance of carefully tended shrubs and tall trees. At the center of the circular driveway in front of the residence, cascades of water flowed perpetually from a carved marble fountain.

After leaving their vehicles, the men regrouped to ascend the stairs to the massive doors of heavy oak that led indoors.

There they were greeted by two uniformed employees who led them into a lavish sitting room with dark teak-paneled walls and ornate antique wood furniture.

"Jesus Christ, are you kidding me?" Mayor Gillette said, as soon as he entered the sitting room. He smacked his fore-head lightly with the flat of his palm.

"He's been like that for years," Jefferies replied, sounding unconcerned, as he came alongside him.

"And he has been very effective through it all," Fagen added as he strolled in behind Jefferies.

Gillette, tall, lean, and very well dressed as befitted a man of means, went over to a portable bar, retrieved a rocks glass and gave himself a healthy pour of vodka.

One of the men who had just arrived—Dale Cummings, the sheriff of Rutland—headed directly to the other side of the portable bar across from Gillette. He lifted a glass and dropped in some ice cubes as he mused aloud, "This guy has been cracking cases in *that* state of mind…"

"Yes," Jefferies said, answering his skepticism. "And some difficult ones involving police corruption. They are *very good* detectives."

"Good detectives, huh?" Gillette said, knocking back his drink. "But isn't one of them just his girlfriend?"

"Yes, that's true, she is," Fagen agreed. "Yet in some important ways she stabilizes Kevin's dissociative identities, so that hopefully this is as far as his personalities fractionate."

"She *stabilizes* Whitehouse? She's a woman. He thinks he's a woman and a Negro? How is that possible?" Gillette ranted, absently holding his glass of vodka up to his cheek.

"He sees what he sees for each individual," Fagen

explained. "He is never challenged as to his gender or race. I don't believe that Margaret is an alter who ever has active control of Kevin. She probably emerged for the first time during the interview, and that's because we threatened her. She came out to warn us—"

Gillette interrupted, pointing his glass at Fagen. "She came *out*? What the hell? She came out from where?"

"Well," Fagen began, "there are some alters who can interact with the outside world. Like Kevin and David. They can take control of the body and do and say things. They can even see each other doing and saying things, and therefore can be in more than one place at a time. But Margaret is an alter—or maybe a group of alters—who has no control over the body she inhabits and is not able to interact with us on a normal basis. Kevin and David see her and interact with her, but it's doubtful that she deals with anyone outside of their psyche."

"What about David's cokehead girlfriend?" Cummings asked.

"I don't know anything about her. She might just be an alter. That's probably how he supplies her without breaking the law," Fagen offered.

Sherman Wells and Vincent Brooks, who had slinked into the room, listened carefully to the conversation, but were too wary to join in. While they were fascinated by Kevin as they watched him through the one-way mirror, and had some questions of their own to ask, their situation was precarious—so they kept quiet. There was a shitstorm of suspicion roiling around anyone connected with Labrec Carville, and the two FBI agents had not only worked with him on several cases somewhat, but he'd introduced them to Richard

Whitehouse in the first place, presently a fugitive from justice.

After refilling his glass, Gillette traversed a wide circle in the room while he harangued his audience. "What I have is a man with mental problems up the wazoo, who has just solved a very ugly case involving the local police chief, the town lawyer, and an expert witness for the FBI..." He stopped momentarily to gaze pointedly at Wells and Brooks. "And we're going to need him to testify in court. How's that going to fucking work?"

"That's not the whole picture," Jefferies asserted. "Carville is already trying to cop a plea. He gave up Harold Klein for the murder of Katherine Werthers right away. They'll put themselves away, for all intents and purposes. And Richard Whitehouse confessed to the killing of William Hamilton and an unidentified homeless man in front of Kevin and Weeks."

Sheriff Cummings sipped from his Scotch and stepped away from the bar. "There also remains the problem of the missing diamonds."

"And how is that a problem?" Jefferies asked.

"You can't be serious," Cummings replied, striking his cowboy hat against his thigh. "Six million dollars' worth of gems cannot be found, Richard Whitehouse vanishes, and his son is the last person to have him in custody. It kind of stinks of collusion."

Jefferies was unperturbed as he continued to defend his reasoning. "According to his own testimony, Kevin wasn't the last to see his father. As David tells it, *he* was chasing him while Kevin was with him, and Richard Whitehouse never got his hands on the diamonds; so there is absolutely no evidence of any dirty dealing involving father and son."

Gillette interjected hotly. "Are you kidding me? Are you listening to yourself, Jefferies? You are asking all of us to believe the testimony of two different people from the mouth of a single individual."

Fagen inserted himself between Gillette and Jefferies, pushing his glasses back from the bridge of his nose. "Mayor, you have to admit, from what you yourself witnessed in the holding room, they are indeed two very distinct people. Three, in fact."

"Admitting and believing are two different things, Doc," Gillette replied.

"What I want to know," Cummings said, "is why Carville would involve Kevin and David in this case in the first place. I realize that initially it was only about Richard Whitehouse's explosive demise, but the idea that he would allow their scrutiny at all is hard to understand."

"Carville felt he had no choice," Agent Wells chimed in from the other side of the room, removing his aviator glasses. "Carville told us that Kevin was digging in deep with or without Carville's approval since he was determined to rule out his father's death as a suicide. The fact that Jefferies vouched for Kevin and David made it harder yet to shake them off."

"I guess he was in a tight spot," Agent Brooks said.

Jefferies scratched at his razor-stubbled cheek. "I don't think he had much of a choice. Kevin and David were already onto something fishy. Carville's only option was to carefully steer them in the wrong direction while keeping an eye on them. It must have drove Carville crazy trying to find David Allerton snooping around. He must have been like a ghost to him."

Gillette frowned. "I have a serious problem with calling them *them*, or *this one* and *that one*. It's a fucking *him!*"

"Yeah, it's a little disconcerting," Cummings added.

"Well, I assure you—" Dr. Fagen started, but a deep sigh from Jefferies interrupted him. "Look, gentlemen," Jefferies explained, "you have six million in diamonds somewhere.

Who knows, Trip Hepner could have unloaded them years ago, or hid them someplace where no one would ever find them. Whatever... it's over. You have your killers, you have your crime solved. What you're digging around for now is a scapegoat."

He paused before adding, "As far as I'm concerned, those two boys can go home and my report will read that the case is closed. If I were the two of you"— Jefferies indicated Cummings and Gillette—"I would channel all my resources into finding Richard Whitehouse, because I strongly suspect he won't stop combing through Brandon, Vermont, until he finds those diamonds. They are his only way out of here, before he is caught or killed."

"So you're washing your hands of all of this?" Agent Brooks asked.

"My hands aren't dirty and neither are any of yours," Jefferies said as he prepared to leave. "Praise the two New York City detectives for solving the case, put the guilty behind bars, bury the dead, and live to play another day, gentlemen. I wish you the best of luck with the apprehension of Richard Whitehouse."

"Jefferies," Gillette called out to him as he started toward the front door.

Jefferies stopped in his tracks, reluctantly. "What?"

"In this world, it takes friends to get by. Sooner or later, everybody is going to need the help of their friends. I just wanted to let you know, you don't have any here," the Mayor said coldly.

"Thank you, Mayor. But you need to remember, New York isn't some pissant town like yours. I doubt I'll ever need your help, but if I do, I would hold some gratitude in reserve for me if I were you. After all, it's on your watch that a chief of police and the town lawyer were found to be corrupt and implicated in at least three murders. The local press will have a field day with this, but imagine the story on the front page of *The New York Times*."

Finished with his parting shot, Jefferies was joined at the front door by Dr. Fagen, and the two left together.

THE FAMILY TIES THAT BIND

The next day, Kevin waited alone outside the motel for his uncle and cousin to pick him up. After they arrived—sunny-faced as usual—Kevin climbed into the front passenger seat; then the three of them watched as the lush green landscape of Brandon, Vermont, melted away as they neared the airport. Minutes after they parked their vehicle, Nick and Paul flanked Kevin as the three walked through the airport terminal. Kevin had flung the small bag across his back by its strap, while Paul pulled the larger one on wheels along behind him.

"So it's back to the big city, huh?" Nick said to his nephew as they neared the waiting area before the gate.

"How about a beer?" Paul asked.

"When did you start drinking beer?" Nick asked him.

Paul laughed. "*You* told me I could."

"I said you could have *one* the last time we went out to dinner as a family."

"Well, I thought you meant that I could drink beer from then on."

Nick shook his head. "We'll have to talk more about this when we get home."

"Awww... c'mon, Pop," Paul pleaded.

Kevin looked at his wristwatch. "We've got some time. Let's go and get a beer for the kid before you kill him tonight, okay, Uncle Nick?"

"Who said anything about killing him? I'm just going to break his neck," Nick said with a big smile, stepping behind Kevin to tousle his son's hair affectionately.

They changed direction to head over to a food and beverage concession, making themselves comfortable on some stools that lined the counter. After ordering three beers, they waited silently to be served, while they watched all the people bustling around them.

Nick noticed that Kevin seemed unusually grim, despite the fact that he and his friend had closed a big case, making them media celebrities in the small town. But Kevin had nothing to say about it as he spent his last half hour or so in their company. Possibly all Kevin wanted now was to escape back to New York as quickly as possible, under the wire and off the radar.

Nick thought then that in some ways Kevin took after his elusive father, who was also standoffish and something of a puzzle. But considering that the two lived on opposite sides of the law, he wondered how the recent ugly revelations about Richard would affect Kevin. Was it this knowledge that made him as mute and introspective as he was now? Nick himself found the news about his brother deeply disturbing, so he could only guess at how much more painful it was for Kevin. No one spoke of Richard's motivation to get involved with the heist though. It was as if the subject was deemed off limits to discussion, especially, it seemed, by Kevin.

"There's going to be a lot of paperwork connected with the funeral," Nick finally said.

"I can imagine," Kevin replied, slowly sipping his beer. "First, I come here because my father is dead, and then practically overnight I find he's alive again—and a thief and a murderer. This was the freakiest shit I have ever experienced in my life, and I live in New York City!"

Paul laughed, grateful for Kevin's sudden levity.

Nick was taken aback, wondering how Kevin could reconcile his feelings so quickly, and express them with some humor. Maybe it was because he was leaving Brandon and putting it all behind him. "Yes, Richard is alive. It's unbelievable," Nick said carefully.

Again they sat in silence drinking their beers.

While watching a group of attractive young women walk by, Paul asked Kevin, "Did Uncle Richard actually get away?"

Kevin turned to his cousin, and thought for a moment about the implications of the question before he replied. "Yes. We tried to stop him, but he had devised a rather clever getaway and it worked."

"We?" Nick asked. "You mean you and David?"

"Yeah, that's right."

"What's a *getaway*?" Paul asked.

"A plan." Kevin replied. "He planned his escape in advance, using a boat."

Nick remarked, "I know that I'm speculating here,

but your father might've gotten away with millions in diamonds."

"No, he didn't," Kevin said flatly.

Nick took a sip of his beer and added, "Well, I'm just saying… *if* he did, we could use a few thousand dollars to pay off a few bills, do some home repairs and get Linda ready for college."

Kevin regarded his uncle with some dismay as he said, "*I* don't have the money, Uncle."

"I'm not saying *you* do. But if you ever meet up with my brother, remind him that he's got a brother."

Kevin chuckled as he thought how preposterous the situation was and turned up his beer for a long swallow.

"And remind him that I'm his nephew," Paul said, laughing.

"If I ever see my father again, believe me, he'll be broke and going straight to jail."

With a tinge of sadness, Nick said, "You think I should be ashamed to ask you this, but sometimes things are not what they seem to be. Who's to say if you did or didn't have some sort of connection with this heist, my brother's escape, and the disappearance of the diamonds? I'm just saying: if any of the Whitehouses benefit, I want to be a part of it."

"That's a pretty cynical statement, Uncle. Are you wired?" Kevin asked with a tight, false grin.

"What are you suggesting?" Nick sat back, touching his chest.

"Are you trying to extract a confession from me?"

"No," Nick avowed. "And I don't know how you could possibly think that of me."

Kevin finished up his beer. "I'm heading to the gate now. It's been nice seeing you guys again."

Nick rose to his feet and said, "Same here, Kevin," as he hugged his nephew.

Paul too gave Kevin a quick hug before they went their separate ways.

As he walked off, Kevin didn't turn around.

"Is anyone sitting here?"

Kevin looked up to see Margaret in the aisle, pointing to the empty seat beside him in the rear of the aircraft.

"You got a ticket on the same plane and didn't tell me?"

"You needed time with your family," she said sweetly.

"Come and sit down."

She slid smoothly into the seat beside him, bestowing a quick kiss on his cheek.

"What's the first thing you're going to do when you get home?" Margaret asked.

"Get into my bed and just sleep."

"How was it being around the family these past few days?"

"You know families. Horrendous."

"Yeah."

"I mean, I really think they might have been wired tonight. In fact, I believe *everyone* thinks that my father found the diamonds and I let him get away with them."

"It does look a little suspicious," Margaret remarked as she ran her fingers back through her hair.

"Thank the dear lord, I have a witness!" He sat back in his seat. "David tried to shoot the man, for fuck's sake."

"David is ex-Special Forces. How did he miss?" Margaret pointed out.

"I don't know. It was dark, the boat was moving, my father was shooting back at him . . ."

"David can shoot the hairs off the ass of a flea, running, diving, and doing his taxes all at the same time."

"Like I said, I don't know."

They fell silent as Margaret rested her head on Kevin's shoulder and closed her eyes.

"Let me ask you a question?" Kevin said, stroking the top of her head. "Do you believe me?"

"Believe what?"

"That I wasn't a part of my father's criminal activities in any way, shape, or form."

Margaret thought for a moment. "Kevin, if you were a part of this, I believe you would have told me. But, in any case, you just don't have any such craftiness inside you—no larceny in your soul. Besides, you have David and me to keep you honest. Why do you ask me that?

"Oh, I just wanted to know whose side you were on."

"Your side—you silly man." She turned her head then to look him full in the face. "That bed of yours sounds comfortable. Mind if I share?"

"When we get home, that's a given," Kevin replied.

Mary Olman opened her door and her face brightened when she saw David Allerton on the other side. A long-haired

brunette, her dark eyes shimmered like polished, black ob-
sidian as she stared up at him with relief and joy.

"Hey, baby," he said in his most satiny voice.

Mary jumped into his arms, hugging him tight. "I swear,
every time you walk out of here I'm afraid you'll be coming
back in a coffin."

"That'll be the day."

She pulled him into her apartment, past the short hall
and into the combination kitchen/dining area. Seated comfortably at a table there was Cheryl, Mary's roommate, holding a cup of coffee, another cup steaming in front of the
empty chair across from her. Cheryl, an attractive blonde
with a short tomboy-like haircut, smiled broadly and said,
"Welcome back, stranger! Where have you been?"

"At a funeral for a friend," David replied. If Mary was a
cokehead, or *snow bunny* by definition, Cheryl was equally
so, being her roommate for years.

"I read what's on the Internet," Mary countered. "You
were the notoriously secretive shooter for the Brandon police department."

David sighed long and hard. "I'm too tired to deal with
the job right now, Mary. I just want to get you naked."

Mary smirked, let go of his hand, and seated herself at
the small kitchen table, picking up her abandoned cup of
coffee. "I'm not getting naked, bud. You're not running all
up in this tonight," she said flatly.

David was slightly miffed, but knew he had the upper
hand. Mary and Cheryl were notorious for haunting the
nightclub scene in the city, cruising for a *'bump'* of cocaine.
Sitting in the apartment tonight for some reason must have

been driving them crazy. "How about after a nice dinner then? Then we go to my place and I get you all naked?"

"Nope."

"How about a special dinner *and* dancing, and then I get you all naked?"

Mary thought about it.

"Shit, David," Cheryl said with a chuckle. "I'll get naked for you for just a smile alone." David knew that Cheryl was partly serious, being that she and Mary would perform sexual favors for their little 'bumps' in the night. Not that she would make such a serious proposition in front of Mary, still David would not put it past her.

"He's not talking to you, Cheryl," Mary reminded her, and both women broke up laughing.

"Okay, David," Mary finally agreed. "If you add some heavy petting, and some vodka along with it, you'll have a naked woman on your hands later tonight. I don't give a fuck whatever else we do."

"I could use it. I need a break before the next crazy-assed case that Jefferies hands us." David pointed off down the hall. "You mind if I use your bathroom?"

"No, go ahead. Why do you even ask?" Mary said, looking surprised.

David left the room, leaving the two women alone.

"He is very hot," Cheryl said once David was out of earshot.

"He's very interesting too," Mary added.

"And you say he acts like he's black?"

Mary nodded, lifting the cup of coffee to her lips. "He acts black every chance he gets."

"He talks black too?"

"Yes, and surprisingly well."

"Well, then when are you going to tell him?"

Mary looked down into her coffee cup. "How do you tell a white man that acts like a black man that his white girlfriend is having his baby?"

FIN

THE STORY CONTINUES...

The Liberians don't forgive or forget. Nor do they have any intention of writing off their losses. They have revenge at heart, and the only one they can train it on is Kevin Whitehouse. While Kevin and Margaret try to simply live their lives together in New York City, David Allerton is feverishly hunting down those who are hunting down Kevin. There is nothing terribly unusual about murder in Manhattan. But when the bodies lead like breadcrumbs to the investigatory trio, the city heats up as the true masterminds make themselves known, in ways more powerful and surprising than the three ever could have guessed. Join us in the continuing saga as the walls close in and death is around every corner in Pale of Darkness, the third volume in the Darkness series.